"Once a snob, always a snob."

"I am *not* a snob!" Abbey told Flynn angrily. "I'm not saying my mother is better than your father, but they don't have anything in common. And the gossip will be unbearable!"

Flynn didn't answer.

"What about you? Are *you* in favor of this marriage?" she demanded.

"Not especially."

"Good," Abbey said briskly. "Now we're getting somewhere. If we cooperate, surely we can bring a quiet end to this engagement before the whole town hears about it."

Flynn eyed her thoughtfully. "You know, you've got a point. Now that we've renewed our acquaintance, I can't think of anything worse than having to face you over the family dinner table every holiday. So you can count me in, Miss Stafford, ma'am. I'll be pleased to break up the old folks' romance."

Leigh Michaels may hold the world's record for the shortest career as a graduate student. She began work toward a master's degree in English on a Monday morning at 7:30 a.m., and by noon she had decided that her future did not lie in studying Chaucer. But it wasn't fear over writing a thesis that discouraged her; it was the fact that Harlequin had just agreed to publish her first book. So she dropped her classes, sold her textbooks back to the bookstore and headed for home to write another romance novel—a decision she has never regretted.

Books by Leigh Michaels

HARLEQUIN ROMANCE
3141—PROMISE ME TOMORROW
3171—GARRETT'S BACK IN TOWN
3184—OLD SCHOOL TIES
3214—THE BEST-MADE PLANS
3233—THE UNEXPECTED LANDLORD
3248—SAFE IN MY HEART

Don't miss any of our special offers. Write to us at the following address for information on our newest releases.

Harlequin Reader Service
P.O. Box 1397, Buffalo, NY 14240
Canadian address: P.O. Box 603,
Fort Erie, Ont. L2A 5X3

TIES THAT BLIND
Leigh Michaels

Harlequin Books

TORONTO • NEW YORK • LONDON
AMSTERDAM • PARIS • SYDNEY • HAMBURG
STOCKHOLM • ATHENS • TOKYO • MILAN
MADRID • WARSAW • BUDAPEST • AUCKLAND

ISBN 0-373-03263-3

Harlequin Romance first edition May 1993

TIES THAT BLIND

CHAPTER ONE

JANICE STAFFORD was already in the big country kitchen when Abbey came down the stairs. She was standing by the long windows looking out over the garden at the back of the house, with a china cup and saucer in her hand. Her mind, however, was obviously elsewhere, for she didn't hear Abbey.

That her mother was up, dressed and drinking coffee at this hour was no real surprise, Abbey thought. Janice had never been the sort to loll around in her dressing gown till noon. But her trimly tailored blouse and crisp flared skirt were not quite what Abbey had expected, either. It was barely seven o'clock.

"High heels? At this time of the morning?" Abbey said, reaching for the coffeepot.

Janice's cup rattled and she turned hastily. "You startled me, Abbey. I expected you'd sleep till noon, after your long drive yesterday."

"I couldn't. The lilacs woke me." Abbey leaned against the sink and took a swallow of the pungent brew.

Janice smiled a little. "They were making too much noise, I suppose?"

"No. My bedroom windows were open, and the smell drifted in, cajoling me. Even burying my head under the pillow didn't help. I'm not used to that, you know. There aren't any lilacs within miles of my apartment. Here, well, how many did Dad plant, anyway?"

"Enough to make a forest." Janice had turned back to the window. "It's only the middle of May, and already the garden is looking ragged," she said almost to herself. "It just gets beyond me."

Abbey shrugged. "So call Frank Granger. He's still taking care of every squeaky closet door and clogged basement drain in the whole neighborhood, isn't he?"

Janice blinked, as if she hadn't thought of that option. "Yes, but—"

"So maybe he'd appreciate a few days of gardening, instead. At least he'd get some fresh air that way."

A big-boned, gray-haired woman came in the back door and let it slam. "I made it," she gasped. "I might be too old to remember what day the garbage is picked up, but I'm not yet so decrepit I can't chase the truck down the street when I see it."

"Too bad you weren't still in slippers and your nightie, Norma." Abbey grinned at the image, then sobered. Norma was showing her age; there was no denying that the wrinkles on her face were deeper than they had been at Christmas. It was at least twenty years since she had come to work for the Staffords, Abbey calculated.

And her mother was beginning to show the marks of age, too, Abbey realized with a whisper of dread. Janice's figure was as trim as ever, but there were fine lines in her face and soft gray streaks in her light brown hair.

Abbey waggled a finger at her mother. "So what's the occasion? Don't tell me you've gone and got a real job, with a time clock to punch and everything."

"No, it's just a meeting of one of my committees again."

"Too blasted many committees," Norma muttered.

Janice ignored her. "I'm sorry, Abbey, I know it's your first day at home. But it is an important agenda today, and I don't feel I can miss it. I honestly thought you'd sleep for hours yet.''

"Don't worry about me, Mom. I'm sure Norma will baby-sit."

Norma snorted. "I'll send you out to play, that's what I'll do."

"It'll be just like old times. I think I'll cut some of those lilacs, if you don't mind, Mom."

"The fragrance is too heavy to bring inside, darling."

"I know. I'm going to take them up to the cemetery." Abbey drained her coffee cup and set it down. "Do we still have some of those outdoor vases, Norma? You know the ones I mean—the metal cups with the spikes attached so they won't blow away."

Norma shot Janice a look. "Try the storage shelves in the basement."

"I'll bet you know where everything in this whole house is," Abbey said admiringly. "What would the Staffords ever do without you, Norma?"

The vases were precisely where the housekeeper had said they'd be, neatly stacked on a set of wooden shelves that ran along one wall of the storage room. Some of them were rusty, and Abbey sorted through the pile, choosing two of the best-looking containers. "Norma's let her housekeeping standards slide a bit," she murmured as she climbed the stairs again. "A few years ago those things wouldn't have dared to rust."

Norma was loading the dishwasher. "Don't leave it too long," she was saying as Abbey came in. "Something's bound to break."

"Norma, please, enough. I'll take care of it. Trust me." Janice handed over her cup and saucer. "I'd better run. I'll be late as it is. Oh, I forgot to tell you, Abbey, we're invited to cocktails at the Talbots tonight. I thought I'd ask Wayne Marshall to pick us up."

She sounded almost hesitant, Abbey thought. That was strange; Wayne Marshall had been a friend of the family for years. "I haven't seen Wayne in months. It'll be fun."

"I have to spend part of the afternoon with Dorothy," Janice mused, "because the arrangements for the summer flower show have to be finished soon. Would you like to have lunch at the country club, Abbey?"

Abbey gave her mother a hug. "It sounds as if that's the only time you have free. Don't panic, all right? We've got the whole summer. Surely every day can't be like this."

"I'll meet you at twelve, then." Janice gathered up her handbag and a cardigan sweater. "Norma, you might tell Frank the faucet in my bathroom is dripping."

"Am I likely to see him today?" Norma muttered. But Janice was already out the door.

Abbey leaned against the row of kitchen cabinets. "My mother is beginning to sound like a dizzy blonde."

"Your mother is lonely."

"Right," Abbey scoffed. "She has absolutely nothing to fill her time. No friends, no activities . . ."

"Staying busy isn't always the same as being happy."

"What do you mean?" Abbey followed Norma into the family room and watched as she began plumping pillows and gathering up newspapers.

But the housekeeper's mouth was a tight line, as if nothing would make her utter another word. Abbey studied her for a moment, then took a different approach. "What might break?" she asked.

"Hmm?"

"A little while ago, you told Mother that something might break and that it shouldn't be left."

Norma gave her a sidelong glance. "One of the oak trees at the back of the garden is dead. It'll have to come out or branches will start falling all over the place every time the wind blows." She switched on the vacuum cleaner.

Abbey relaxed. "And you don't think Mom will remember? You could always call the tree people yourself," she said over the roar of the motor. Then she turned to leave. "I'll be back in an hour or so, Norma."

The dew still hung heavily on the lilac bushes, and Abbey gently shook each branch as she cut it. Spring was further advanced here in the Midwest than it had been in Minnesota; the deep purple blossoms were almost completely opened, and the earliest of the blooms were starting to wither.

Lilacs were not really a spring flower at all, Abbey's father had always said, but the first signal of summer. This year that signal was particularly welcome to Abbey, for she would have the whole summer at home. The whole summer free...

No, not free exactly, but the two long years of her teaching fellowship were over, and she could begin looking for a permanent position—one that wasn't limited to instructing college freshmen on how to write paragraphs and topic sentences. And in the meantime, she had the whole summer to complete her research and finish writing her dissertation.

The whole summer. She stretched in sheer delight. It would be a treat to set her own hours for a change.

It was likely to be the last summer she'd be able to spend at home, though, for a permanent university position meant that next year there would be other demands on her. It made the coming months even more precious to know that they'd probably not be repeated.

Her basket heavy with fragrance, Abbey opened the gate and let herself out of the garden, then started down the path. Little more than a depression in the thick grass, the walkway twisted through the middle of the block of houses where an alley would have been if this exclusive neighborhood had possessed anything so plebian. It skirted the back lawns and flower beds, staying the maximum distance from the houses themselves but making neighborly visits easy. It had been that kind of neighborhood as long as Abbey could remember—full of people who were friendly without intruding on one another's privacy.

"And yet," Abbey muttered, "they all know everyone's business as surely as if it was published in yesterday's newspaper!"

But she said it with fondness. This five-block stretch of Armitage Road, with its big expensive houses and well-to-do inhabitants, had become her world when she was five years old. She could barely remember the little bungalow on the other side of town where they had lived while Warren Stafford struggled to establish his law practice. It was from the big brick Tudor-style house on Armitage Road that she had gone off to school for the first time. It was here she had learned to ride a bicycle and where she had broken her arm the day she had tried to rescue the Campbells' Persian cat from the Austins' maple tree. . . .

The Campbells had put in a swimming pool, she saw, and next door the Powells' colonial had a gleaming coat of fresh white paint. Abbey could judge precisely how fresh it was because the shutters hadn't yet been reinstalled and were stacked in piles on the brick terrace. One was balanced on a pair of sawhorses, and bending over it, whistling a tune, was the neighborhood handyman.

Frank Granger was practically a natural resource on Armitage Road. If anyone needed a drainpipe cleaned, a load of junk hauled away, a shelf put up, an outlet re-wired, a window unstuck, they called Frank. The man could do anything he turned his hand to, and there was no job he was too proud to take on. And he never, ever, breathed a word about anything he might see as he moved from house to house.

And if sometimes one had to wait days for Frank to come, well, what of it? There was no one else who could handle the kind of odd jobs he could, not for minimum pay and without complaint.

Abbey had been afraid of him when her family had first moved to Armitage Road. Frank Granger not only didn't gossip, he seldom spoke at all, and for a long time Abbey had almost believed the deliciously scary tales the older kids told about why Frank didn't talk.

She smiled at the reminder of her own innocence, as she cut across the grass toward the sawhorses. The Powells wouldn't mind if she trespassed for a minute; all the residents of Armitage Road took advantage of any opportunity to catch Frank when they needed something done.

He looked up as she approached, and his whistle died. But he didn't speak, just stood there quietly with a screwdriver in his hand. She wasn't surprised; it had always been his habit to wait till he was addressed.

"Hi, Frank. We've got a dripping faucet, whenever you've got time to look at it." She perched on the edge of a brick planter. It might take a few minutes to get a commitment from Frank; she might as well be comfortable while she waited.

He pushed the screw into the hole he had drilled and worked it deep into the wood. Once it was firm, he looked up again and said quietly, "Did your mother send you here to talk to me?"

Abbey shook her head. "Not exactly. I was on my way to the cemetery, and when I saw you, I thought I'd take care of it for her."

His gaze flicked over her; his eyes, deep-set in his heavily tanned face, were a startling shade of pale clear blue. Then he turned back to the shutter and picked up another screw. "I heard you were home," he said.

"That's Armitage Road for you. I just got in last night, but I imagine the whole neighborhood knows."

"You're going to take it easy for the summer?"

"It's not a vacation, really. I'll be doing research at Chandler College for my doctorate." What had got into the man? she wondered. He was being positively chatty!

"You're a teacher now." It was not a question.

Abbey nodded. "English literature."

"Shakespeare and all that? That's interesting. I'll have to tell Flynn."

Abbey blinked, unable to imagine why Frank thought his son might be interested in anything Abbey Stafford was doing these days.

And I certainly don't recall Flynn Granger taking any particular interest in literature, either, Abbey thought. At least not the kind that didn't include centerfold pullouts!

"What's Flynn doing these days?" she asked. It was merely good manners. She hadn't seen Flynn Granger since their high-school graduation ceremony, and it wasn't likely their paths would cross again.

"Painting." Frank lifted the shutter off the sawhorses and set it aside. He was a tall man, but there was nothing bulky about him, and it surprised Abbey a little that, despite the shutter's size and obvious weight, he moved it without apparent effort. "Too bad he's not around to-day."

Abbey glanced at the gleaming white clapboards. Flynn wasn't a bad painter, but then, he would have learned from his father.... Frank must have painted every room in every house on Armitage Road over the years.

"I'm sure we'd enjoy talking about old times," she agreed with only the barest hint of irony.

Frank looked up from the pile of shutters with a flicker of appraisal in his eyes. "I'd forgotten. You never did run around in the same crowd, did you?"

That, Abbey almost announced, was the champion understatement of the year. Abbey Stafford and Flynn Granger as bosom buddies? Hardly. She had been an honors scholar and president of the student council, while Flynn had been class clown, almost expelled once because of graffiti on the wall of the girls' locker room. And why he'd chosen that particular location for his handiwork was anyone's guess.

"No, we didn't spend much time together," Abbey agreed. "But maybe I'll run into him while I'm home."

"No doubt." Frank didn't look up from his tape measure. "He's right in the neighborhood, you know. He lives at Mrs. Pembroke's place now."

"What?" Abbey's astonishment overrode her good manners. Flora Pembroke's stone manor house was one of the original mansions on Armitage Road, squarely in the center of the most desirable block. If Flynn Granger was in that sort of league all of a sudden ...

The drill stopped whirring and Frank said, "He has the chauffeur's quarters over the garage."

Abbey started to breathe again. Fool, she told herself. If Flynn Granger had won the lottery and Flora Pembroke sold him her house, Janice would certainly have mentioned it. "That must be a great help for Mrs. Pembroke."

"Yes, Flynn's right there whenever she needs a hand. You're taking the flowers up to the cemetery, you said?"

Abbey glanced at her basket, which sat almost forgotten at her feet, and nodded. "Lilacs were my father's favorite." They were wilting a bit as the dew evaporated, she realized. She stood up.

"He's been gone a long time, now," Frank said.

Abbey didn't have to calculate. "Six years next fall," she said. "I was just starting my second year of college. It doesn't feel like that long, of course." She picked up the basket. "Oh, when you come to check out Mom's dripping faucet, Frank, you might take a look at the garden, too. She told me she'll be needing help with it, so you might want to give her an estimate."

"I'll think about it," he said. He didn't look up from the replacement slat he was fitting into position.

She shook her head ruefully as she walked on up the winding path. She'd forgotten how independent Frank Granger was. Once, a home owner new to Armitage Road had made the mistake of telling Frank she wouldn't trust him with a key. Not that Frank had fussed or made a scene. He just became too busy to help Mrs. Miller out ever again.

And Flynn was just like him, Abbey thought. She had never realized before that Flynn had inherited his irritating habit of shrugging off authority and going his own way, no matter what the consequences. It was too bad, really; that sort of attitude closed a lot of doors.

The sun had burned off the dew by the time she reached the cemetery. But the grass, newly washed, was brilliant emerald, a perfect foil for the soft gray and red and white of the tombstones scattered across it. Abbey filled her vases with water from the outdoor faucet and placed them carefully at the corners of the big white marble monument, then sat cross-legged on the grass as she arranged the lilac boughs.

It was peaceful here. By the faucet, a couple of blue jays squabbled over the water she'd spilled, and far off in the row of pines she heard the call of a blackbird.

It had not been so peaceful on that autumn day six years ago when she had first come up to this hillside. It had been threatening rain, and the wind had whipped Abbey's long blond hair and tugged at Janice's raincoat as they stood hand in hand, each holding a single red rose to be placed on Warren Stafford's grave. It was the only goodbye they could say. He had been barely fifty, and men that age were not supposed to drop dead in the middle of a summation to the jury, with no warning and no second chance.

His death had been a bitter blow to them both. It was years before Abbey could come here and sit calmly, accepting the reality that life went on even though her adored father was gone. And as for Janice, who had buried herself in committees and projects . . .

She's lonely, Norma had said this morning.

"Of course she is," Abbey muttered. "But if Norma is suggesting that the answer might be another man . . ."

Was that what Norma had been implying? Surely not. No one could replace Warren Stafford in Janice's life or heart.

And yet, there had been that moment this morning when Janice had mentioned Wayne Marshall. She'd sounded odd, almost as if she was testing a new concept, tiptoeing around it until she could see how Abbey would react.

No, Abbey told herself. It was crazy even to think it. Wayne had been her father's longtime friend, that was all. There was certainly nothing romantic between him and Janice. And as for the idea of Wayne's escorting Janice to the Talbots' cocktail party, well, Wayne was the head of the psychology department at Chandler College, and Janice chaired the alumni fund-raising committee. There was nothing unusual about their going together to a cocktail party given by the college's president.

It certainly wasn't a date.

THE COUNTRY CLUB had been closed for a while that spring, Janice had written, so the dining room could be redecorated. But her mother's letters hadn't quite prepared Abbey for the change. The dark club-room atmosphere was gone, and now the rooms were open and light and airy. The dining-room hostess showed her to a small corner table, draped in green and ivory, and brought her a cup of coffee while she waited for her mother to arrive.

But it wasn't Janice who came across the room to greet her a few minutes later. It was Wayne Marshall. He gave her his usual enthusiastic hug—or was it more restrained than usual? Was it her imagination, or was there a question in his eyes?

"Will you join us?" she asked. "Mother will be along any moment now, I'm sure."

"Oh, no, I've got a meeting with the manager. In any case, I'm sure your mother wants some time alone with you. You've got things to talk about and all that."

Abbey said slowly, "Wayne, is my mother all right?"

"Healthy, you mean? Of course she is. She's just fine."

She shook her head. "I'm not sure what I mean. She seems different somehow than she was at Christmas. No, the change has come since then. She wasn't like this at spring break when she came to see me."

Wayne sighed. "Give her a chance, Abbey. She's got a lot on her mind."

"Like what?" Abbey asked baldly.

He hesitated, and in that instant Janice Stafford called from across the room, "Wayne! You came, after all."

He turned to her with a smile. "Not really, dear. I just stopped to say hello to Abbey."

Why should that simple statement sound almost like a warning? Abbey wondered.

"I'll see you later tonight, all right?" He glanced at Abbey, kissed Janice's cheek and said softly, "I'll be at home this afternoon if you need me."

Janice nodded. He pulled out her chair, let his hands rest for a moment on her shoulders, then left.

"I presume he meant in case you want his help with the plans for the flower show." Abbey picked up the menu and stared at it.

Janice laughed. "Heavens, Wayne doesn't know a gladiolus from a peony, Abbey. The taco salads have been wonderful lately, and they've got a new sandwich, too. Here it is." She pointed to the menu. "It's like a chef's special, a little of everything, but he calls it 'debris on rye.' It's delicious."

"Then that's what I'll have." Abbey handed her menu to the waitress and leaned back. "These chairs are wonderful. The whole place is terrific, as a matter of fact. Have you been seeing a lot of Wayne?"

Janice shrugged. "A fair amount, I suppose. We've been on a couple of committees together lately."

"Do they meet in the afternoons at his house?"

"Abbey!"

"Mother, you must admit that sounded like an assignation."

"It's nothing of the kind. Wayne is a very helpful person when one needs advice—or comfort."

She sounded almost like a lost child, in desperate need of counsel and consolation. Abbey let her eyebrows raise slightly, but stayed silent.

Janice toyed with her soup spoon and studied the single iris in the centerpiece. Then she took a deep breath and said, "There's no easy way to tell you, I suppose. All right, full speed ahead and damn the torpedoes, just as Wayne advised. I'm going to be married, Abbey."

Abbey had just picked up her water glass; it tipped sideways from her suddenly nerveless hand, and icy liquid splashed across the linen tablecloth and onto the deep plush carpet. Two waitresses and the hostess converged with cloths and towels; it was all Abbey could do to mutter an apology.

Still, the fuss gave her half a minute to compose herself. Why should it be such a shock? she asked herself. She herself had been wondering, no more than an hour ago, if Janice might be thinking about dating again.

But that's different from marriage, Abbey thought helplessly. *To have already decided... To break it to me like this... To do it so suddenly!*

But perhaps it wasn't altogether sudden from Janice's point of view, she reflected. Perhaps she had deliberately kept quiet until she knew that this new relationship was serious.

Or perhaps it wasn't sudden at all. Wayne Marshall had been Warren Stafford's friend forever, and Janice's from the day of her wedding. Perhaps he had fallen in love with her then, and waited patiently for her. He had certainly never found any other woman to his liking, or he'd have married long ago.

If this was what Janice wanted, well, it wasn't the end of the world, was it? Six years was a long time, and of course Janice was lonely. If she could find happiness once more with Warren Stafford's good friend, who was Abbey to tell her she shouldn't?

She gathered her shattered composure. "I can't say I'm exactly thrilled, Mother, but I'm sure I'll get used to the idea."

Janice reached across the table and squeezed Abbey's hand so tightly it was almost painful.

"Now I know why Wayne didn't tell me himself," Abbey murmured.

Janice smiled. "He knew it would be a shock to you. He said to tell you that if you wanted to talk it over..."

Abbey nodded. "Of course. That's why he's staying home this afternoon. It's a shock, yes. But I like Wayne, so I'm sure it won't be hard to get used to him being around all the time."

Stop babbling, Abbey told herself. *It's not as if you're twelve years old and acquiring a full-time stepfather, for heaven's sake.*

Janice's quiet voice cut across her thoughts. "I'm sorry, Abbey, but you've misunderstood. It's not Wayne I'm marrying."

Abbey swallowed hard. "Not Wayne?"

"No. He merely meant if you needed to talk to someone, as a friend—"

Abbey interrupted ruthlessly. "Then who?"

Janice's smile was uncertain, almost wobbly. "Frank," she said softly. "I'm marrying Frank Granger."

CHAPTER TWO

IT WAS ABBEY'S early training that kept her sitting in her chair. If it hadn't been for the rules of proper conduct that Janice had drilled into her all the years of her childhood, Abbey would probably have stood up and pushed the table over, or started throwing crystal and cutlery.

The bitter irony was that the woman who had made such a point of the need to be a lady was the same one who had just announced she was marrying the neighborhood handyman. And she had chosen the country-club dining room—a bastion of society in which Frank Granger had probably never set foot—to do so!

It was also understandable, Abbey decided. Janice had chosen her time and place deliberately, knowing very well that no matter how much Abbey wanted to throw a tantrum, she wouldn't do it in the country-club dining room. That early training was far too strong.

The waitress brought their sandwiches. She set Abbey's down with particular care, as if she half expected the plate to be bounced across the room like a tiddledywink the moment Abbey touched it. Abbey stared at the open-face sandwich, hardly seeing the layers of roast beef, tomato and avocado.

Debris on rye, Abbey thought. What a perfect name for the whole occasion! They were surrounded by wreckage—a soggy table, a wounded mother-daughter relationship, a damaged mind...

That was it. Janice had flipped, that was the only answer.

"Abbey, when did you start adding cream and sugar to your coffee?"

Abbey looked down at her cup. She hadn't been aware of doing anything, but her coffee was definitely not black anymore. She picked up her spoon. "Just since you announced you've gone crazy," she said. "Mother, what in heaven's name inspired you to fly off on this tangent?"

Janice sighed. "Please try to understand, darling. I still miss your father, and I always will. But he's been gone for a long time, and I've been lonely—"

"Lonely I can understand," Abbey interrupted. "What I don't understand is why you think Frank Granger is any cure for loneliness. He's never said more than twelve words to anyone in his life."

Though if she were being honest, she had to admit that Frank had been quite talkative—at least for Frank—this morning. She'd noticed it at the time and wondered why. Now she knew. He'd been trying his best to impress her, to win her approval.

Abbey sighed. "You haven't announced this, have you?"

"Of course not."

Her mother sounded almost offended at the idea. That was a blessing; perhaps Janice hadn't told anyone because deep down inside she knew what a crazy idea it was. If that were the case, she might be nudged back to her senses *if* Abbey went about it right. And *if* she could collect some support from Janice's friends....

"Obviously Wayne knows," Abbey mused, "though I'll never believe he wholeheartedly approves."

"Wayne wants me to be happy."

Abbey directed a level stare across the table. "Are you implying I don't?" she asked softly.

Janice's gaze dropped to her sandwich. "No, darling. I understand that it's a shock, and that you might not understand why I've chosen to do this."

That, Abbey thought irritably, was an understatement. "If I honestly thought it would make you happy, Mother... But Frank Granger!" She sighed. "Who else have you told? Not that I'm planning to take an opinion poll or anything. I'd just appreciate some warning about where I'm likely to run into discussions of your plans."

"Norma knows, of course."

"Of course." The remark Abbey had overheard this morning had far more meaning to her now. *Don't leave it too long,* Norma had said. *Something's bound to break.* It was obvious now that it was this news she'd been talking about, not a dead oak tree in the yard!

"Well, she could hardly avoid knowing."

"And just why is that?" Abbey demanded, suddenly suspicious. "Has Frank been sleeping over?"

"Abbey, don't be ridiculous!"

"You're blushing, Mother."

With determination in her voice, Janice returned to the original question. "Norma knows, and Wayne. And Flynn, of course."

"Oh, yes," Abbey murmured. "Flynn. I can just about imagine what Flynn thinks of this."

"That's everyone who knows. We didn't want to make a general announcement until we'd told you, so don't jump to the conclusion that I haven't broken the news to my friends because I'm afraid of their reaction, Abbey."

Abbey bit her tongue. That was exactly what she had been thinking, but of course notifying her daughter first was the sort of courtesy one could rely on from Janice.

Still, no matter how much Janice protested, Abbey was not convinced that her mother was honestly unafraid of her friends' reactions. Janice wasn't naive.

"And now that you've broken it to me? Is it going to be in tomorrow's paper, with your picture and all?"

"Of course not, Abbey."

There was a note of annoyance in Janice's voice, and Abbey seized on it. "No announcement? All right, Mother, confess. It's something else entirely that's wrong, but you were so afraid I'd be furious about it that you're softening me up by giving me this ridiculous story about marrying Frank Granger."

"Abbey—"

"It's like when my roommate told her parents she was dating a cannibal so when they found out she was really only flunking biology they could keep it in perspective. Right?"

Janice didn't even smile. Very softly she said, "Abbey, I'm marrying Frank Granger."

Abbey put her fingertips to her temples. Her whole head felt like a hand grenade with the pin pulled, just waiting to explode. "Mother," she said quietly, "I think we'd better take this up later. I really can't deal with any more right now."

Janice nodded. "I understand. Will you at least talk to Wayne?"

"I'll think about it." Abbey pushed her chair back and stumbled out of the dining room.

The sun was still shining; the sky was cloudless. But the morning's promise of the perfect summer had vanished, and the fresh air threatened to choke Abbey.

She drove around aimlessly for nearly an hour. If she went home, Norma would instantly know what had happened, and Abbey didn't want to hear her views on the subject.

She wasn't ready to talk to Wayne, either. He would no doubt try to bring her around to Janice's point of view, but she was certain he couldn't honestly approve of her mother's plans.

Janice herself had as much as admitted that. *Wayne wants me to be happy,* she had said, not *He thinks it's a great idea.* And it was obvious that Wayne had anticipated Abbey's reaction. Such insight certainly indicated that Wayne, too, had his doubts and shared that reaction.

And what sane person wouldn't have? Abbey asked herself. It was ridiculous to think of Janice Stafford, with her degree in philosophy, settling down happily with a man who mended toilets for a living. It was ludicrous to picture Warren Stafford's widow, accustomed to opera and symphony and ballet, living with a man who probably thought the banjo was the best musical instrument ever made.

"My father could have been a Supreme Court justice if he'd lived," Abbey said under her breath. "They discussed the finer points of law over dinner every night. And the man she wants to put in his place..."

It was too much. She turned toward home, hoping to slip past Norma and retreat to her room. But as she passed Flora Pembroke's house, she saw someone working in the flower beds at the side of the old stone manor. It was definitely not Mrs. Pembroke, unless Flora had grown a good twelve inches and taken a decidedly masculine turn.

What did Flynn Granger think of this? Abbey found herself wondering. Janice hadn't said anything about his reaction. Did that mean he, too, was opposed? It wasn't what Abbey would have expected from him, but still...

"It certainly can't hurt to find out," she said aloud, pulling into the drive.

When Abbey came around the corner of the house, Flynn turned his head, and for a moment his hands stopped moving among the canes of the rosebush he was tying to a trellis. Then he turned back to his task without a word, as if he fully intended to ignore her.

Abbey leaned against the warm stone wall and surveyed him. It had been years since she'd seen Flynn, but she would have recognized him anywhere. There weren't many men with hair so dark that the sunlight picked up blue highlights in the windblown strands. And his eyes, the deep blue of a perfect day on the ocean, had an unusual slant that wouldn't change, no matter what his age. But other things about him were different, of course. The tall, skinny, often clumsy boy had become a lean solid man with no lack of coordination or muscles....

Especially muscles. That was obvious, for Flynn was wearing leather gloves, jeans and boots, but nothing else. The jeans, so old they were worn soft and pale, rode low on his narrow hips, and Abbey could see the taut ridge of stomach muscles under the dark hair that tapered down across his chest to his belt.

She dragged her gaze back to his face. He had stopped working and was standing, head turned and eyebrows raised, watching her. His narrowed eyes—much darker than his father's—seemed to be summing her up.

Abbey said quickly, "Doesn't Mrs. Pembroke mind you running around half-naked?"

"Oh, no. In fact she approves, because lots of people stop by now who never used to find time for her." His voice had changed, too—it was deeper, lower, softer. "When was the last time you visited Flora, anyway?"

Abbey's jaw dropped. "Flynn Granger, if you're implying I only stopped because I spotted your body and couldn't control my urge to drool over you . . ."

"I'm not implying anything."

"That's better."

"But thanks for the compliment. You could have said you were offended by the sight, you know. But obviously that wasn't what you were thinking at all." He turned back to the rosebush. "I see the happy news is out."

"Your father and my mother?" There wasn't any point in fencing around the subject. "Personally, I'm not thrilled."

"Somehow I expected that."

"And what does that mean? That you're in favor?"

Flynn shrugged. There was a corresponding ripple of muscles in his back. "My father is a big boy. I figure he can make up his own mind on things like this without my help."

"So you are in favor." Abbey watched his hands moving surely among the thorns. "I suppose you're planning to move into the family mansion right along with him."

"Why would I? I have a perfectly good place here."

"Tending flowers for Mrs. Pembroke and living above the garage? Come on, Flynn."

"It's not a bad part of town. Somebody once said that the young man on his way to success should maintain an elegant address even if he lives in the attic."

"Somehow," Abbey said dryly, "I expect whoever it was meant the attic of the house. The space over the garage is a few steps lower."

Flynn shrugged again. "Still, it's on a Armitage Road."

She glanced around at the garden. Flora Pembroke had always been known for her elaborate floral displays, and the roses looked particularly fine this year. "And it's close to work."

"That's an advantage, too. So where do you live?"

"Minneapolis."

"I know that. I mean, do you have a house in the ritzy district, or what?"

"I've been sharing an apartment with a friend. What's it to you?"

Flynn shook his head. "You don't even have a place of your own? My place might only be a garage, but it's all mine."

Abbey gave it up as hopeless. "Look, I really didn't come here to talk about your garage, you know. Don't you even care that this marriage is going to make your father look like a prize fool?"

"Marrying above himself, you mean?" There was an odd twist in his voice.

"That's not what I mean, but you must admit it's certainly going to look odd. And the talk will be unbearable."

"For whom? You?" Flynn gave a little snort. "At least you're true to form, Abbey. Once a snob, always a snob."

"I am not a snob! I'm not saying my mother is better than Frank. I just don't think they've got anything in common. Certainly not enough to keep them happy if he's not comfortable with her friends. Good Lord, Flynn, what's he going to talk about to the neighbors? Their clogged drains?"

"If that's what they want to discuss."

"How long is that fascinating subject going to last?"

"How about your mother? What is she going to talk about with his friends?"

"My point exactly. Though as far as that goes, my mother is a perfect lady. She can talk to anybody about anything."

Flynn didn't answer.

Abbey let the silence drag out for as long as she could stand it. "Aren't you afraid those thorns will swing back on you and scar your precious tan?" she asked finally.

"Not as long as I'm paying more attention to them than I am to you."

"Great. Thanks. I'm glad this is so important to you." She paced six steps down a garden path and back. "Why do they want to get married, anyway?"

"Are you here again?"

"I'm not going away till I understand. If they're such good pals, why can't they just leave it at that?"

Flynn stopped working and turned to level that deep blue gaze on her. "Surely you don't think people their age aren't still interested in having sex on a regular basis, Abbey."

"If you're not going to be helpful, Flynn—"

"You said you wanted to understand."

"Thank you, but I do not need any explanation of the facts of life."

"So what *do* you want?"

"Do you like the idea of them getting married?"

"Not especially. I don't know Janice all that well, but I'm inclined to agree she's not quite the right person for my father."

Abbey frowned. That wasn't quite the way she had phrased it, but perhaps it didn't matter. "Good," she said briskly. "Now we're getting somewhere. If we co-operate, there's a good chance we can make them see they're being foolish, and bring a quiet end to this before the whole town hears about it.''

"Oh, I can't wait to hear your plan."

"I'll have to work it out." She looked at him suspiciously. "Wait a minute. You wouldn't be planning to double-cross me? Find out what I intend to do and then warn Mother and Frank?"

He pulled his right glove off with his teeth and held up his hand in the standard I-swear-to-tell-the-truth position. "Of course not."

Abbey wasn't convinced. "A few minutes ago you weren't exactly violently opposed."

He put the glove back on. "I wasn't exactly in favor, either. Besides, a few minutes ago I hadn't truly renewed my acquaintance with you."

Abbey glared at him. "What has that got to do with anything?"

Flynn eyed her thoughtfully. "Because now that I have, I can't think of anything worse than having to face you over the family dinner table every holiday." He finished tying up the last rose cane and leaned over a small lawn mower to pull the starting rope. "So count me in, Miss Stafford, ma'am. I'll be pleased to help break up the old folks' romance."

FLYNN GRANGER was impossible, she fumed. But then, he always had been. To be perfectly fair, Abbey admitted, he generally hadn't set out to be a troublemaker. Nevertheless, wherever Flynn went, trouble followed.

It had been Flynn who had filled the high school with smoke from an unauthorized chemistry experiment, and Flynn who had shaken the whole community when he reviewed *Ulysses* for the student newspaper. Abbey couldn't count the number of times she had seen Frank waiting in the school office for yet another discussion of what to do about Flynn.

Her personal problems with Flynn Granger went back further still, to the days when he had tagged along Armitage Road in his father's shadow. For instance, there was the time he'd chased Mrs. Campbell's Persian cat up the tallest maple tree on the street. Abbey had heard the poor creature mewing piteously and, filled with compassion and righteous wrath, started up to rescue it. That she had tumbled out of the tree and broken her arm in three places was not exactly Flynn's fault, she supposed; still, she could never quite forget that he'd been the indirect cause of it. The fact that the cat had made its own way down—unscathed—before Abbey's cast was even dry, didn't excuse his behavior, either.

And it looked as if things hadn't changed much in the intervening years. Running around Flora Pembroke's flower beds half-naked—what kind of a handyman was he, anyway?

One point in Frank's favor, she decided, was that even at his most iconoclastic moments he had always been fully clothed when he was working on Armitage Road.

Flynn Granger was trouble from the word go, and if it weren't absolutely necessary to have his assistance, she'd have kept her distance. But the situation was too important. Her mother's happiness was at stake, and if she had to cooperate with Flynn to save Janice from herself, so be it.

She spent the afternoon on the deep window seat in her room, staring out the casement windows, idly tracing a fingertip over the swirls and flaws in the old glass panes and thinking up one plan of attack after another.

Precisely fifteen minutes before Wayne Marshall was to pick them up for the Talbots' cocktail party, she tapped on the door of her mother's room.

Janice was sitting at her dressing table, fastening a diamond earring. She turned as Abbey came in, and the light from the big French doors leading onto the terrace sparkled off the sequins that accented the lines of her black dress. Abbey recognized the dress; Janice had bought it in Minneapolis just a few months ago, when she had come up to visit Abbey during spring break.

She looked fragile, Abbey thought, also wary and tired. Would it be better, she wondered for a split second, not to fight this marriage? To do as Wayne had and wish Janice happy for the moment, no matter what the long-term consequences?

Janice brushed a hand over the sequins and said, "You look startled. Is it a bit too much, Abbey? I probably shouldn't have bought this, you know. There isn't much need for fancy dresses here."

If Janice Stafford had few occasions for a sequined cocktail dress, Mrs. Frank Granger would have a lot less, Abbey thought grimly, and bit her tongue to keep from telling her mother that she might as well get the good out of the dress in a hurry. Yes, she reflected, she was doing the right thing in trying to bring Janice to her senses.

"It's a great dress, Mom," she said, keeping her voice light. "I knew the minute you tried it on that it was perfect for you."

"Well, things look different in the city sometimes."

"Trust me, it's lovely." Abbey pulled a small needle-point stool close to her mother and sank down on it, her jade-green skirt forming a pool around her feet. "I wanted to tell you how sorry I am for making a scene at lunch, Mother."

Janice blinked.

"I'm sure you understand what a shock it was," Abbey murmured. "Still, that doesn't excuse my going to pieces like that."

Janice softly brushed the back of her hand against Abbey's cheek. "Of course it was a shock for you. But I'm sure when you've had some time to think about it..."

Abbey seized the opening. "Of course I'll adjust, given half a chance. I'm awfully glad you haven't set a wedding date yet, you know, and you're not going to announce the engagement immediately."

Janice looked a little doubtful.

Abbey plunged on. "It will make things so much easier for me if I can get used to the idea myself, before there are all kinds of comments and opinions from everyone else in town. It's so thoughtful of you, Mom, to consider me like this, delaying everything for my sake."

Janice opened her mouth as if to protest, then closed it.

"In fact, I'm looking forward to getting to know Frank better," Abbey continued. "Will he be there tonight?"

"At the Talbots' party? Oh, no..."

Abbey looked down at her hands, folded primly in her lap, to hide her satisfaction. "How silly of me. Of course cocktail parties aren't really Frank's style, are they?"

She sneaked a glance at her mother. Janice's eyes had narrowed suspiciously.

Don't overdo it, Abbey warned herself. *Change the subject fast and get out.*

She stood up with a graceful swirl of jade-green silk and looked around for something else to talk about. "What a pretty box." Her fingertips caressed the walnut jewel case that sat on the corner of Janice's dressing table. She probably would have admired the box no matter what it looked like, but it really was a beautiful thing. It was slim and delicate, with gracefully rounded corners and an intricate rosebud carved in the top. The carving was shallow, because there was no room for more, yet the flower seemed to have real depth. She dropped a kiss on her mother's cheek. "I'll let you finish dressing, Mom. Wayne will be here any moment—he never keeps a lady waiting, does he?"

She was out of the room before Janice could possibly have had time to wonder if that last comment was a dig at Frank. And though Abbey was breathing rather fast as she ran down the stairs, her hand light on the polished bannister, she felt pleased with herself. The first phase of her new plan had gone well. Tomorrow she'd have to hunt Flynn down again—making it look like an accidental encounter, of course—and fill him in. But that wouldn't be difficult; the Pembroke house was right on her way to the campus. She'd simply walk over to Chandler College to start her research, and on the way she would surely see Flynn out working in Flora Pembroke's garden.

Wayne Marshall rang the bell precisely on the dot. Abbey answered the door and offered her cheek to be kissed. "Mom hasn't come down yet. You'll have to make do with me for a minute or two."

His eyebrows lifted warily. "You sound in awfully good spirits, everything considered."

"Why shouldn't I be?" She remembered something Flynn had said and decided to put it to use. "My mother is a big girl. She can make up her own mind about things like this without my help."

Wayne's eyes lit with warmth and he squeezed her hands. "Abbey, I knew you wouldn't make trouble."

Guilt trickled through her veins like ice water. "I didn't say I liked it," she warned.

Wayne nodded. "Of course you've got your doubts. That's only natural. It's a big change for Janice—and for you."

"Well, don't you have doubts?" Abbey challenged. "Honestly, Wayne, if she wants full-time companionship, there are a lot of people around this town who are more likely candidates than Frank Granger."

Wayne looked thoughtful. "At a glance, yes."

"And after a long look and a hard stare, too, I'd say." Abbey sighed. "Take you, for instance..."

How much more appropriate Wayne Marshall was, she thought. How much more pleasant it would be to share life with someone like him. No one ever had trouble talking to him, while she couldn't think of a single subject she could confidently bring up with Frank Granger. If Janice had only had the good sense to choose Wayne, instead....

Abruptly Abbey realized how far she had come since that morning, when she would have announced with assurance that Janice would never marry again at all, that her devotion to Warren Stafford had been so complete she would never consider another man in her life, not even Wayne Marshall!

"Your mother and I have always been good friends, Abbey," Wayne said.

"Far too good to let romance ruin things," Janice agreed from the lowest step. She came forward with hands outstretched, her eyes sparkling.

Abbey drew a deep breath, then told herself firmly that she was imagining things. She had seen her mother greet Wayne hundreds of times. This time was no different.

Five minutes later, and just three blocks up Armitage Road, they reached the front door of Ashton Court, the French-provincial-style mansion that had been turned into a cultural center for Chandler College a couple of years ago. The Talbots lived in a newly remodeled apartment on the upper level, but the party tonight was downstairs, in the gorgeous public rooms.

Abbey wouldn't have missed the party for the world. She hadn't been in the massive house since its conversion, and she was intrigued by the changes. She tried to keep her attention firmly on Chandler's president as he brought her up-to-date on the college's new developments, but her gaze kept straying to the art on the drawing-room walls, which she was itching to examine more closely, and finally Dave Talbot laughed and waved her off.

"Go get yourself a drink and wander around all you like," he said fondly. "And stop by my office sometime in the next few days, and we'll talk business where there's nothing to distract you. I hear from your mother that you're in the market for a full-time position."

Abbey nodded. "I've started sending out my applications."

He looked concerned. "It's a bit late in the season to be trying for a job with a university, Abbey. Most of them have already hired for the autumn."

"I know I'm late, but I wanted to be sure my dissertation would be done so I can give full attention to a new job. With luck and all of Chandler's resources, I should be wrapping it up by August."

"Well, perhaps someone will have a sudden vacancy. That happens, you know. I'll keep my ears open, if you like."

"Thanks, Dave. I'll stop in to see you." Abbey drifted off toward the bar, which had been set up at the end of the drawing room, and paused to study the painting hanging above the fireplace. It was an abstract in vibrant primary colors, and Abbey thought it looked like two women working on a motorcycle. She read the little card placed discreetly to the side, stating the name of the artist and what the painting represented. The description didn't make much sense, so she finally gave up and leaned against the bar, thinking what a change that painting was from the honest-to-goodness Seurat that had hung there when Ashton Court was a private home.

The bartender turned to her and reached for a glass. "What can I get you, Abbey?"

She blinked once and told herself it was silly to be surprised; Flynn could turn up anywhere, and he wasn't exactly out of place behind a bar at Ashton Court. With a crowd like this, Cynthia Talbot must have had a terrible time finding enough people to help. "Tonic water," she managed to respond. "And I need to talk to you."

He filled the glass and passed it across to her. "Likewise. But let's make it later, all right? Things will let up soon and I can take a break. Besides, you don't want to be seen hanging around the bar."

"Why? Because people will think I'm a sot?"

His smile flashed. "Or besotted, perhaps," he suggested, and turned away to mix a martini.

With him? It was just as well he wasn't looking, Abbey thought. Sticking her tongue out was not proper behavior.

She strolled through the rooms, greeting old friends and catching up on news and gossip. There was plenty of both, and Abbey couldn't help wondering what it would be like if Janice's incredible news ever got out. The story would travel like an epidemic, that was sure, and it would probably get more outlandish with every telling. She tried to stifle a shiver.

It was almost an hour before Flynn was finally free, and he casually worked his way across the crowded dining room toward her. The sleeves of his white shirt were still rolled to the elbow, but at least he'd straightened his wine-red tie. His pleated dark gray trousers weren't nearly as body-hugging as the old jeans he'd been wearing in the afternoon, but they were just as attractive.... Abbey realized abruptly that she was staring.

Rather than continue to watch him approach and take the chance that someone might wonder why she was suddenly so interested in Flynn Granger, Abbey turned her back to him and looked up at the nearest painting, a watercolor that hung above the antique sideboard.

A tiny tingle in her bones warned her the moment he arrived. She kept on staring up at the painting, rather than look at him.

"Fascinating, isn't it?" Flynn murmured.

She wanted to giggle at his proper art-gallery tone, but as a matter of fact he was right. "It's marvelous," she agreed soberly. "It's unusually dark and rich for a watercolor."

"Absolutely. It was also unusually well received. It won the Reynolds purchase award last year for 'best in show' at the Chandler art festival. That's why it's hanging here."

"Really?" She peered at the corners of the painting to look for a signature, since the tiny information card was blocked from her view by a large woman wearing a huge feathered hat. She couldn't find one. "Who painted it?"

"I did," Flynn said. "But enough about art. You wanted to have a chat. While nobody's looking, shall we slip out for a walk?"

CHAPTER THREE

FLYNN'S HAND SLID gently under her elbow, and before she could argue, Abbey found herself going out the French doors onto the terrace. Not that she minded, exactly; the dining room had got uncomfortably warm all of a sudden.

Flynn was painting, Frank Granger had told her just this morning. And Abbey, looking at the fresh white paint on the Powell's house, had jumped to conclusions.

"Oh, murder," she said. "How could I have forgotten that it wasn't the words you wrote on the wall of the girls' locker room that got you into such trouble, it was the caricatures?"

Flynn grinned. "Someday they'll wish they'd preserved that wall, instead of painting over it." He tucked her hand into the bend of his elbow and looked doubtfully at her shoes. "Are you game for a stroll through the gardens? They've done the paths over, but . . ."

"I'll struggle along. Though I'd have thought you'd have had enough of gardens for one day. Why do you spend your time weeding Flora Pembroke's flowers, anyway? And don't tell me it's because you can't turn paint into hard cash." She waved a hand vaguely toward the house. "There must be a market for work of that quality."

"Now and then. Still, it's not exactly steady. So Flora rents me the garage for a pittance, and I help out when I have time. She's happy to have a man around. I'm happy not to have to hold a regular job."

Abbey thought it over and nodded. "I see. It's a good-Samaritan deed."

"Well, don't go telling everyone that." He sounded disgruntled. "I'd hate to have my bad-boy image ruined."

"Don't worry," she said crisply. "I still haven't forgotten about Mrs. Campbell's cat, you know."

"Don't blame me. I told you the stupid animal would come down by itself when it got good and tired of being up there."

"But the real point is why it was up in the tree in the first place, don't you think?"

"Abbey, it doesn't matter anymore. The cat's been dead for years."

"No doubt driven to suicide by your persecution."

"I'd say it's more likely that he choked to death on an especially fat robin."

She blinked. "He ate robins?"

"Only when he couldn't catch bluebirds and goldfinches," Flynn said grimly. "The more exotic the bird, the tastier he seemed to find it. That particular day, I seem to recall, it was a whole nest of baby cardinals."

"Oh."

"But that's all water over the dam. At least, I assumed when you said you needed to talk to me that you didn't mean to take up the case of Mrs. Campbell's cat yet again."

He didn't need to be so self-righteous about it, Abbey thought. "No, it was Mother I wanted to talk about. But you go first."

"My father stopped by this afternoon and told me what a charming young woman you are."

"He did?"

"It was only then that I realized the scale of the delusion we're dealing with. What's your plan?"

Abbey stifled the urge to sock him in the jaw. Instead, she dug a much-folded pamphlet from her tiny evening bag and handed it to him.

He squinted at it; twilight had fallen, and here among the big trees it was almost dark. "What's this?"

"It's Chandler's calendar of cultural events," Abbey said impatiently. "I'm going to ask Mother which concerts and recitals she plans to attend, and then I'll suggest we make a party of one of them. Maybe a buffet supper after the symphony concert next Saturday night, if that's not too soon."

"And?"

"And I'll invite Frank. She'll think I'm trying my best to make him feel welcome, but she'll have to notice when he falls asleep in the middle of Beethoven's Ninth, don't you think? Or when he's miserable at dinner and uncomfortable with her friends?"

Flynn sounded doubtful. "She'll take you seriously? I mean, she won't figure out what you're up to?"

"Of course she'll take me seriously. I've used classic reverse psychology on her. I even apologized for the way I reacted when she broke the news. Now, you see, I'm in a position to quietly cast doubt without ever openly disagreeing."

"I thought you were looking awfully pleased with yourself."

"And this way, when she decides to break it off, she'll honestly think it was her own decision."

"All from one party." Flynn sounded unconvinced.

"Not completely, but when she actually sees him in those surroundings rather than alone, she'll have to start asking herself if she isn't being a fool. It'll take some time of course, and I'll have to be on my toes every minute to keep her believing I'm really on her side, but—''

"You're going to humor her," Flynn said thoughtfully, "and every chance you get, you'll point out the flaws in her thinking—and in Dad—as if they're advantages."

"That's it."

"Just as she no doubt did to you when you brought home unsuitable dates."

"Flynn, I never dated anyone unsuitable."

"Oh, that's right. You always hung around with the good boys from the right families. I'd forgotten how very boring you were."

Abbey gritted her teeth and let that one go by. "In the meantime, I've won another victory. I talked her out of announcing the engagement, or setting a wedding date."

"So?"

"So," she said impatiently, "the delay gives us a chance to act."

"And time for your party to show her how clearly Dad doesn't fit in with her life-style."

"That's the basic idea."

He rubbed his chin. "Abbey, exactly how do you plan to illustrate to Janice that this engagement is unsuitable if you're still trying to keep it secret from the whole world?"

Abbey shrugged. "All I'm doing is inviting Frank to a party. Mother's not blind. I won't have to hit her with an ax. It's just that she's obviously never seen him in those surroundings."

"And you honestly think that my father turning up at your mother's party isn't some kind of public announcement?"

"All right, you come up with something better!"

He thought about that for a moment. "If I do, you'll help?"

"Absolutely."

"I'll work on it."

They solemnly shook hands on the agreement and started back toward Ashton Court. More time had passed than Abbey had realized, and the cocktail party was breaking up. Cars were pulling out of the parking lot at the back of the house, and people were milling around, waiting for friends. Fortunately no one seemed interested in one more couple slipping out of the shadows.

"Maybe it would be better if we don't go in together," Abbey said.

"Right. See you around," Flynn said casually, and turned away.

"Flynn!" Abbey's voice was urgent, and even as he wheeled to face her, surprise flaring in his eyes, she told herself she was being silly. What good would it do to ask him for reassurance, anyway? Even if she got a promise that everything would be all right, she wasn't likely to believe it! She heard herself saying quietly, "Why didn't you tell me years ago that Mrs. Campbell's cat was killing birds?"

For a moment she thought he wasn't going to answer, but finally, softly, he asked, "Would you have believed me years ago?"

He melted into the shadows at the side of the house. She watched him go before she climbed slowly to the terrace.

"Abbey!" Janice called from the open French doors in the dining room. "There you are. I thought you'd vanished."

And before Abbey had a chance to sigh with relief that her mother hadn't spotted Flynn, Wayne Marshall chuckled. "What a picture of family togetherness that was—you and Flynn walking along with your heads together. Charming sight."

Janice said with a laugh, "Abbey always used to tell me how much she wanted a big brother."

Heaven preserve us. Abbey bit her tongue just in time. Flynn Granger for a brother? He was the last person on earth she'd choose to fill that role!

WITH THE SPRING SEMESTER over and another week to go before the first summer session began, the Chandler College campus was practically empty. Abbey had had the library almost to herself for three days, and she was grateful for the quiet coolness of the special-collections room. Outside it was unseasonably hot and noisy, as paving contractors rebuilt the street that skirted the campus. But inside there was only the hum of the climate-control systems and the distinctive scent of old books to interfere with her concentration.

At least, that was the way it should be, Abbey told herself for the thousandth time on Thursday afternoon, as she pulled her attention back to the sixteenth-century manuscript lying open in front of her. She'd been staring at it for nearly an hour, and she hadn't the vaguest idea what the faded intricate Elizabethan script said or if it had any bearing at all on her chosen subject.

Chandler College possessed the Midwest's most extensive and exclusive collection of original Elizabethan materials, she reminded herself. She was lucky to have entry to them at all, and especially the kind of access she had been granted. Because of the fragility and rarity of the books and manuscripts, there were rigid rules regarding their use. But Abbey had begged for, and been granted, the privilege of rummaging through the stacks to see if there might be something that didn't show up in the catalogs or lists, but that might throw light on the obscure English poet she was studying.

And what was she doing with her precious library time? She was thinking about the evening ahead, when Frank Granger was coming for dinner!

Abbey tossed her pencil aside with a groan and put her face in her hands.

The door opened, and the young professor who had unlocked the room for her hours earlier peered in. "Abbey, I hate to disturb you when you're working so hard, but..."

She looked up. "Is it closing time already?"

Sara Merrill came into the room. "Not quite. But it's so warm in my office that I'm ready to call it a day. Do you mind if I close the collection down early?"

She looked concerned, quite ready to put herself out so that Abbey could manage another half hour of work.

As Abbey thought of her nonproductive afternoon, she felt a wave of guilt wash over her. Sara might just as well have taken the whole day off; it wouldn't have made any difference to Abbey's dissertation. "No, that's fine."

"If you're at a bad point, I can just wait outside. There's always something I want to read, and the air-conditioning is on in the library, classes or no classes." She made a face. "Over in the liberal-arts buildings, we have to conserve energy any time the students aren't around. I don't know why I bother to stick it out here in the summers."

Abbey managed a smile. "I suppose someone has to do it."

"Well, I didn't mean to say you were a nuisance. You've been so quiet I almost forgot and locked you in."

"Oh, please, don't do that. I've had such a terrible time concentrating today I'm ready to go home." Even if she had to face Frank there, she almost added. She began to gather up her notebooks.

Sara smiled. "I know. It's incredible, isn't it? The effect this room has, I mean. It's not my favorite period of literature, but I still come regularly just to breathe in the atmosphere."

Abbey nodded, feeling even guiltier. It was true enough that a fan of literature and history could overdose just by looking around this room, but it was hardly fair of her to take credit for being sensitive when her preoccupation came from another source altogether.

Tomorrow, Abbey told herself firmly as she began trudging home, she would settle down to serious work. It would be easier to concentrate, anyway, once this first awkward evening was out of the way.

And no matter how hard all three of them tried, it was bound to be uncomfortable, she thought gloomily. Perhaps, as soon as dinner was over, she could excuse herself and leave her mother and Frank to a quiet evening....

Maybe that wouldn't be such a bad idea, she realized on further consideration. It would certainly make the point, subtly but definitely, that while she was prepared to be polite to Frank, she hardly found his company fascinating. She quickened her pace, feeling marginally more cheerful.

That, of course, was before she spotted the motorcycle parked negligently beside the back door of the Stafford house. She looked at it thoughtfully for a long moment, then took a deep breath and went inside.

Janice, in a calico apron, her face flushed a delicate pink, was checking a casserole in the oven. Flynn was leaning against the breakfast bar drinking a soda. There was no sign of Frank, but the kitchen table was set for four with colorful calico place mats and casual stoneware dishes.

Abbey eyed the table and her mother's apron with concern. In Abbey's entire memory, Janice had never served a guest more than a cup of coffee at the kitchen table. And even when it was only the three Staffords sitting down to dinner together, meals had always been served in the dining room, with linen and china and Grandma Stafford's sterling silver flatware.

If Frank Granger had convinced Janice to change her habits so radically and if he had encouraged this sudden turn to domestic pursuits...

Good heavens, Abbey thought. Bringing her mother back to her senses might be more difficult than she'd bargained for.

"Where's Norma?" she asked.

"She went out to a movie with a friend."

"Leaving you stranded with dinner guests?" Abbey poured herself a glass of iced tea. "That's not like Norma."

"I'm not stranded, Abbey. I am perfectly capable of cooking a simple meal. Anyway, Norma has been taking a little more time off lately. Her doctor told her to slow down."

Flynn raised his eyebrows at Abbey as if to say, *That put you in your place, didn't it?*

Abbey glared at him, unwilling to admit anything of the sort. At least his soda was in a glass with ice. It was some comfort that the Grangers hadn't yet managed to convert Janice to serving soft drinks straight from the can.

Janice put a plate of asparagus in the microwave and whipped off her apron. ''Bring the tossed salads out, would you, please, Abbey? They're in the refrigerator, all ready.''

''I haven't even changed.''

''Oh, just wash up, honey. This is nothing fancy. I'm going to see if Frank's finished yet.''

''Finished?''

''Fixing my faucet.'' Janice disappeared up the back stairs.

''Well!'' Abbey said.

''Don't blame me for the informality.'' Flynn was studying the ice cubes in his glass. ''I offered to wear white tie and tails, but your mother insisted it would make you uncomfortable.''

''It certainly would.'' She fixed him with a stern look and moved to the kitchen sink to scrub her hands. ''Mom didn't say anything about inviting you.''

''To a little family get-together? Do you honestly need notice and a guest list?''

''Maybe you didn't think you needed an invitation.''

''Come on, Abbey. You can't believe I was so eager to come that I invited myself.''

''I wouldn't put it past you.''

He shook his head. ''I think Janice was afraid of creating sibling rivalry if she favored you and left me out.''

''Not a chance,'' Abbey muttered. Over the splash of water, she added, ''This is utterly ridiculous. They can't get married.''

Flynn shrugged. ''So how's the master plan shaping up?''

''It's all set—after the symphony on Saturday.''

"Am I invited?"

"Of course. I couldn't possibly do without you, could I?"

"How wonderful to be needed," Flynn murmured. "Mind if I get another soda?"

"Make yourself at home."

He grinned, and Abbey, a little late in realizing the implication, rolled her eyes.

Having Flynn there made a difference, though Abbey couldn't quite make up her mind whether he was helping or hindering her. Over dinner, he certainly helped smooth the conversational path, but she wasn't sure that was an advantage. It might have been more useful in the long run if there had been painfully extended pauses while everyone tried to think of a new subject.

But that would never happen, Abbey reminded herself. Janice Stafford was too much of a lady to allow her dinner-table conversations to go sour no matter what the circumstances. So, since it wasn't likely Abbey could make any points during the meal, she decided she might as well sit back and enjoy her food.

"I think Janice was right," Flynn said, looking directly across the table at Abbey.

If having to face her over the family dinner table was such an unpleasant prospect he would do nearly anything to avoid the situation, he certainly hid it well, she found herself thinking. He looked positively happy about it at the moment.

Belatedly she realized that some sort of answer was expected. What was it he had said? That Janice was right? Just what was Flynn up to, anyway? "About what?" she asked with a warning frown.

"She can certainly cook," Flynn said contentedly.

Frank added, "This is good, but wait till you taste her pot roast."

Janice glowed. "Cooking isn't a skill one forgets, you know. It's like riding a bicycle."

Abbey watched her thoughtfully. She'd have said that Janice would have cheerfully gone the rest of her life without setting foot in the business end of a kitchen again. Certainly in all the years Norma had been a part of their lives, Janice had never seemed to mind keeping her distance from range and oven. Now all of a sudden she was sounding like the homemaker of the year. Frank's influence, no doubt.

Glumly Abbey studied her plate. The rich chicken-and-rice casserole no longer tasted quite so good.

Relax, she told herself firmly. Getting the urge to make a pot roast once in a while was no sin. It certainly didn't mean Janice Stafford was ready to give up all her other activities for the dubious pleasure of cooking three meals a day for Frank or anyone else. She was a solid part of the community foundation, the inner circle that kept things functioning. Anyone could cook, but it took someone special to fill the shoes Janice had assumed.

"How did your research go today, dear?" Janice asked.

"About as well as I expected. I didn't find anything."

"And that's going well?" Flynn asked. "What are you researching, anyway? Black holes?"

"I suppose you could say that a poet so obscure he's almost unknown is something of a black hole in literature, but in fact—"

"*I'm* not likely to say it," he interrupted. "It sounds a little too flowery for me. Besides, if the poor man is so obscure, why not just let him rest in peace? If his stuff wasn't good enough to survive on its own merit..."

"It's apparent you never paid any attention in English class."

"I did, too," Flynn complained. "I even sort of liked the stuff that rhymed."

"Things like 'Roses are red, violets are blue'?" Abbey said gently.

"Abbey, honestly," Janice murmured, and Flynn grinned in triumph. "And you, too, Flynn," she went on. "Both of you sound like children."

"Don't you wish you had us around all the time?" Flynn asked.

Janice smiled. "Fortunately the Fifth Amendment says I'm not required to answer that. You'll join us for the symphony Saturday, won't you, Flynn? And for our small party afterward?"

"I wouldn't think of missing it," Flynn said earnestly. "With Abbey doing the planning, it's likely to be the most interesting party of the year."

Abbey had already kicked him under the table before she realized it hadn't been a particularly smart thing to do. What if she had missed Flynn and kicked Frank or her mother? Fortunately she knew she had hit her mark, because Flynn was sending her accusing looks and shifting uncomfortably in his chair as if he'd like to grab his injured ankle. Or kick back.

She found herself wondering glumly if she were likely to have any manners left by the time this was over.

After dessert, Flynn volunteered to do the dishes.

"How noble of you," Abbey said with irony.

"Oh, you're going to help," he assured her. "Don't worry, I won't be the only one getting gold stars for my cooperative spirit." He turned to Frank and Janice. "In fact, why don't you two go for a walk or something? The way Abbey and I have been chattering, you've hardly said a word to each other tonight.''

Janice glanced at Frank, who nodded. "All right. If Wayne phones, Abbey, please tell him I'll call back.''

She took a sweater from a hook by the door. A moment later, as Abbey started to scrape dishes at the garbage disposal, she saw them walk slowly past the kitchen windows. Janice's head was bent and Frank's hands were in his pockets. And neither of them were talking.

"Good for you," Abbey said.

"What? Sending them out to play?'' Flynn delivered a stack of plates to the sink. "I thought you'd be mad at me for throwing them together.''

"Not at all. How are they going to get tired of each other if we keep them apart? But it was a grand idea to point out that they haven't said a word to each other all evening.''

"And that we noticed,'' Flynn added. "Does this salad dressing go back in a bottle somewhere?''

"No, just set the pitcher in the refrigerator. Your father was so nervous he couldn't wait to get out of here. I wonder what he'd have been like if we'd made him sit in the drawing room.''

"Are you certain it's the house that makes him nervous?''

Abbey started putting plates in the dishwasher. "You're surely not implying it was my presence that caused his discomfort,'' she said sweetly. "He thinks I'm charming. I have it on the best authority.''

"I knew I shouldn't have told you that. Still, if you're going to call me the best authority... You wouldn't like to put that endorsement in writing, would you? I may need a résumé again someday.''

She hefted the dripping dishcloth in one hand and looked at him speculatively.

"Don't do it. I retaliate." He took the cloth away from her, wrung it out and moved to wipe off the table.

"They weren't even holding hands," Abbey mused.

"And you're disappointed? I thought you wanted them to be discreet."

"It just surprised me, that's all."

"I've got it. I'd better run a check on Janice. Maybe she's blackmailing him, and that's why there's no lovey-dovey stuff going on."

"Blackmailing Frank? Into an engagement? You know, you might be right. She probably wants to marry him for his money."

Flynn shrugged. "Well, he does have a skill that's in demand. At least they'll never starve. And if she's happened to lose all her money playing poker or something . . ."

"They simply can't get married," Abbey said drearily.

"Why not? They're free, sane and of legal age."

"Because . . ." She shook her head in despair and said rather wildly, "For one thing, I've got no idea what to give them for a wedding present."

"Abbey, I hate to break this to you, but—"

"Oh, it's easy for you. Just put a swirl of watercolor on a piece of paper and sign your name. Five minutes and you're done."

She wasn't looking at him, and so she missed the way his mouth tightened momentarily into a straight, almost hard line.

"But it's not so easy for me," she went on. "We'll just have to stop it, that's all. How's your plan coming along, by the way?"

"It's on hold," Flynn said coolly.

"What kind of collaborator are you, anyway?"

He leaned against the counter. "There's no sense in wasting my poor efforts till you've had a chance to try, is there?"

She thought for a moment, not quite certain why he sounded a bit sarcastic.

"And I'm sure if we need a backup plan, I can whip something up in a hurry," he added dryly. "Five minutes and I'll be done."

Abbey winced. "Oh. I hurt your feelings, didn't I? I didn't mean I don't appreciate your work or don't understand the effort that goes into it. That was just a manner of speaking. I mean, it's obvious they'd like one of your paintings. But what on earth else they could use—"

She was interrupted by the chime of the front doorbell, its rich tones floating through the house. Abbey hastily dried her hands. "I'll bet that's Wayne. He's not safe to talk to, by the way. He's managed to convince himself that this whole thing is a great idea."

But the person on the doorstep was no one Abbey had ever seen before, and she studied the young man with caution in the glow of the porch light. He didn't look like a salesman; the portfolio in his hand was leather. Although he was wearing an open-necked shirt and a sweater, he didn't look the casual type, either; there was something about the crease in his trousers that said this man spent most of his time in a suit. And his haircut was very conservative—the style favored by bankers and attorneys.

He was studying her just as intently, and the interest in his soft brown eyes was unmistakable. After a full thirty seconds of silence, Abbey said, "Well? Can I help you?"

The young man blinked. "Oh. Yes. Is Janice at home?"

"I'm afraid not."

He looked disappointed. "I'm Boyd Baxter. I'm an associate with Stafford and Hall, and—"

"My father's law firm?"

"You must be Abbey. I thought so. You look like Janice, you know."

"So I've been told." Her voice was cool.

He flushed a little. "I'm sure you have. I've brought some papers for your mother."

Abbey eyed the portfolio with suspicion. What was Janice up to now? Rewriting her will? Setting up a trust? Arranging a prenuptial agreement? Filing for bankruptcy? But that was ridiculous, and she reminded herself briskly not to pay any attention to Flynn's wild flights of fancy.

"If you'd like to leave them . . ." she began.

"Actually, if I could have just a minute with her. . . Are you expecting her home soon?"

Abbey bit her lip. Janice hadn't said anything about expecting this young man, but the fact he was here in the middle of the evening indicated this was important. Perhaps Janice had good reason for conducting her legal business outside regular hours and public offices.

"I don't think she'll be gone long," she said finally. "If you'd like to wait . . ."

Boyd Baxter nodded eagerly, and Abbey showed him into the big drawing room at the front of the house, turning on the soft lights that spotlighted the paintings and opening the French doors onto the terrace.

He looked around and gave a satisfied sigh. "I've always thought this is the most elegant room in town." He put the portfolio down on the white linen couch and went to stand beside the gleaming grand piano. "Do you play, Abbey?"

"Once upon a time I did. Not lately, and never particularly well, I'm afraid. May I get you a drink while you wait? Or a cup of coffee?"

"Coffee would be wonderful, if it's not too much trouble."

He looked a little like a spaniel puppy, Abbey thought, with those big, soft brown eyes. "I think there's still some in the pot."

But the instant Abbey walked into the kitchen, Flynn was just plunging the glass coffee carafe into the dishwater.

"Gee, thanks," she said. "Now I'll have to make a fresh pot."

His eyebrows went up as he surveyed the empty doorway behind her. "For whom? The invisible man?" He rinsed the carafe and handed it to her, still dripping.

"Boyd Baxter, with some papers for Mother. I left him in the drawing room."

"Why?"

"What do you mean, why?" She spooned ground coffee into the basket. "I could hardly bring him into this little domestic scene—unless you'd care to explain the whole thing to him."

Flynn shrugged. "If he's Janice's lawyer, he probably already knows."

The stoneware they used for everyday was on the handiest shelf of the cabinets, but Abbey stretched to get a china cup and saucer down, instead. "Well, don't feel you have to stick around and be bored with his company."

Flynn folded the dish towel with precision and hung it to dry, then reached for a stoneware mug. "It's all in the call of duty," he murmured. "Janice will thank me for staying, I'm sure."

"You don't have to entertain him."

"I'm not planning to try. I'm just going to chaperon."

Abbey felt herself start to burn. "I don't need a—"

Flynn shook his head sadly. "You're trying a little too hard to get rid of me, you know. What is it about Boyd you found so instantly attractive, I wonder? Well, it doesn't matter. Hurry that coffee along, can't you? It's rude of us to keep poor Boyd waiting."

CHAPTER FOUR

ABBEY DIDN'T EVEN TRY to answer; it was painfully apparent that, whatever she said, Flynn would have a comeback. So she lifted her chin and walked out.

He called after her, with just a hint of laughter in his voice, "I'll be in with the coffee as quickly as I can. Don't let Boyd get impatient—or anything."

Abbey growled a little under her breath.

Boyd jumped to his feet when she came into the drawing room. Abbey forced herself to smile. "The coffee'll take just a minute."

"I didn't mean to cause any trouble." His eyes were even more spaniel-like.

She waved him back to his chair and settled into the corner of the couch. "Coffee's no trouble."

"No, I meant ... if I'm interrupting something ..."

Abbey's face began to feel like cardboard. It was obvious that Boyd had heard what Flynn had said. And equally obvious that Flynn had intended him to hear; his voice had been pitched to carry down the long hall. "Nothing except the dinner dishes, believe me," she said stiffly, and made a mental note never to play chess with Flynn. He'd probably be deadly at that game, too.

Boyd's fingers nervously tapped the leather portfolio on his lap.

"How long have you been in town?" Abbey asked.

He seized the question with visible gratitude. "Just a couple of years. I wanted to get back to the Midwest after I finished at Harvard, and your father's firm had a tremendous reputation in labor-relations law. A national reputation."

"Does it, still?" The question was honestly curious; Abbey knew her mother held a financial interest in the law partnership, but Janice seldom said anything about it. Without Warren Stafford's dynamic presence, Stafford and Hall could easily have slumped into an ordinary small-town practice.

Boyd looked half-shocked at her ignorance. "Oh, yes! Mr. Stafford brought in terrific people, several of whom are now partners. Of course none of them can claim to take his place. He was the expert. It's such a shame, because we could all have learned a lot from him."

It would have eliminated a lot of other problems, too. If Warren Stafford were still alive, Janice would be here in the drawing room pouring coffee. Frank Granger would probably be repairing someone's faulty dead bolt, and Flynn might be almost anywhere at all, but he would certainly not be hovering over the dirty dishes in the Staffords' kitchen. But there was no sense in wishing for the impossible.

Boyd went on earnestly. "This position was perfect for me. I feel very fortunate to have been selected."

Abbey pulled her mind back to him. "And we're lucky to have you. But don't you miss the excitement you had around Boston? There's so much to do there."

"I haven't time to miss it, I'm afraid, because the practice is so busy. Of course I travel a great deal, and wherever I am, I try to take advantage of the things that aren't available here."

Abbey nodded. "My father did that, too. Mom often went with him, and they always took in opera and ballet and theater."

"How about you?"

"It was rare that I could go along. School and my activities interfered." Her gaze drifted to the grand piano. "I wish I'd been with them the night they heard Sol Abrams, though. It was his last concert."

Boyd's tone was reverential. "I've got all his recordings, but it's not the same as hearing him in person, of course." He sighed. "But really, Abbey, this town has an amazing number of advantages."

"No traffic jams," Abbey agreed.

"Yes. But there's the college, for instance. Chandler's reputation is growing at a phenomenal rate. And the space. In cities, it costs millions to own a house like this on a couple of acres—but I understand your father bought this place when he'd only been in practice a few years."

Abbey laughed. "That's true. But he did it on a very stringent budget."

"Of course, I wouldn't expect to be able to do the same thing just now. But someday—" he looked up at the sculptured plaster ceiling and the carved molding that bordered it "—someday, when I've established myself as a partner..."

A cheerful voice from the doorway said, "Abbey, you might want to check out that coffeepot—it's getting slower with every cycle." Flynn had found a small wooden tray; neatly arranged on it were two of Janice's treasured china cups and saucers and one stoneware mug, all full of gently steaming coffee.

He set the tray down on the low table near the couch. Before Abbey could even curse her shortsightedness in choosing to sit there, he'd planted himself firmly in the center of the couch, right beside her, and put a cup and saucer into her hand.

"You take your coffee black, I suppose?" He held out the other china cup to Boyd, who had jumped to his feet.

Boyd took it hesitantly. He was trying not to stare, Abbey thought, and doing a bad job of it. She could hardly blame him; Flynn's making himself at home at the Staffords was a startling development.

"I take it however I can get it actually," Boyd said.

Flynn waved a generous hand at the tray. "Cream and sugar right there," he said. He wrapped his long fingers contentedly around his own large stoneware mug and took a swallow.

"You could have had a china cup, too," she muttered. "It would have looked better."

He gave her an intimate smile. "I was sure you'd want me to be comfortable." And suiting action to words, he settled back into the couch cushions as if he never intended to move again.

Abbey shrank into her corner. The couch was not a large one, and Flynn seemed to take up a great deal of room. With determination, she said, "What sort of house would you like, Boyd?"

Flynn shot her an admiring look. "My goodness, you've made fast progress," he said under his breath.

Boyd leaned forward. "I've always had a passion for these grand houses." He smiled self-consciously. "The one that's always appealed to me most is Ashton Court."

"Too bad for you that the college already has it," Flynn said unsympathetically. "But I suppose you'd be willing to settle for a Tudor-style place—like this one?"

Now Abbey glared at him.

"Oh, this house is wonderful," Boyd said. "But actually any house along Armitage Road would do."

"I thought it might," Flynn murmured.

Boyd frowned at him. "It's the atmosphere of the neighborhood I find really appealing."

Flynn nodded. "The elite aroma of success."

Boyd said rather stiffly, "That's quite true. The character of the street—"

Abbey decided it was time to take a hand. "I know what you mean. The campus changes, and the town does, too. Even the individual houses are altered now and then, like Ashton Court. But Armitage Road just goes on quietly being itself."

Flynn shifted his coffee mug to his other hand. "That's right. Armitage Road doesn't change. It absorbs. In fact, it consumes differences, then processes them and spits them back out in its own approved mold."

Abbey frowned. That wasn't at all what she'd meant, and Flynn knew it. "I would think," she said tartly, "if that's what you believe, you'd be anxious to get out of the neighborhood, Flynn."

He smiled at her lazily. "Oh, but you forgot. I live on the back side, so I'm not really part of Armitage Road at all, even though I've got the prestigious address. Every up-and-coming young man should be sensitive to things like that."

He smiled at Boyd; it was an expression that displayed more teeth than humor.

"Yes," Boyd said. He glanced at his watch. "I suppose I could just call Janice tomorrow about the details. It's only some lists for Chandler's alumni fund-raising committee, and I hate to bother her so late at night, but I have to fit things in when I can. I really haven't time for the committee at all, but one does meet a lot of people that way."

"I'm sure Mother won't mind you waiting for her," Abbey assured him.

Flynn drained his mug and set it back on the tray with a flourish. "There's no need to be in a hurry, Boyd. I have to be going myself, so you might as well stick around and keep Abbey company till Janice comes back. Don't get up, Abbey. I know my way out."

The drawing room seemed very quiet for a full minute after he left.

So much for Flynn's fascination with chaperoning her, Abbey thought. The only thing Flynn had wanted was information, and as soon as he got it he was off. He'd obviously brought up her supposed instant attraction to Boyd just to give himself an excuse to stay and to throw Abbey so far off balance she wouldn't notice what he was up to. But it hadn't worked—not as well as he had hoped, at least. What *had* Flynn expected, anyway? Had he been afraid of what Boyd might tell her or of what Janice might be planning? And why hadn't he hung around in case the committee paperwork was only one part of Boyd's business with Janice?

Boyd said awkwardly, "I'm sorry. I had no idea I was intruding."

"Intruding?" Abbey's tone was almost absent-minded. "On Flynn and me? I couldn't be less romantically involved with Flynn Granger if he were the man in the moon."

Boyd smiled suddenly, and the soft brown eyes came to life. "I'm glad," he said simply. "I saw you at the Talbots' cocktail party a couple of days ago, you know. I didn't know who you were then, but something about you made me want to know you better."

The admiration in his eyes sparked a little glow deep inside her. He was a dear, Abbey thought. There might be some rewarding moments this summer, after all—despite the trouble with the Grangers.

SHE HEARD JANICE and Frank come in the back door a few minutes later and went to warn her mother of Boyd's visit.

They didn't look like a couple in love, Abbey thought as she caught her first glimpse of the two of them. There were no dreamy eyes or slightly flushed faces to imply there had been a passionate interlude outside. And the good-night kiss they exchanged was really only a brush of the lips, the kind of caress Janice's crowd passed around all the time. The whole goodbye couldn't have been more brisk if Abbey had choreographed it herself; in fact, it looked to her as if Janice was eager for Frank to be gone so she could talk to Boyd.

Not that Frank seemed to notice. He merely wished Abbey a pleasant rest and went off into the night, whistling.

Abbey shook her head as she locked the door behind him. So much for Flynn's suggestion that Janice and Frank were no different from a couple of hot-blooded kids eager to sleep together!

Abbey yawned as she went up the back stairs to her own room. It had been a long and wearing day, and she was dead tired.

But she couldn't settle down. She had just turned on her bedside light again and picked up a book when she heard the front door close and Janice's step on the stairs. There was a soft tap on her door and her mother called, "May I come in, Abbey?"

"Of course." Abbey piled her pillows against the headboard and pulled herself up straight.

Janice was carrying her shoes. Had she been trying to sneak down the hall to her own room? Abbey wondered.

Janice caught her glance at the low-heeled pumps. "My toes hurt," she said wryly. "I should have changed shoes before going out. Frank can walk me off my feet even without an extra handicap."

Abbey didn't quite know what to say to that, so she looked down at her book and toyed with the corner of a page.

"Well?" Janice said.

Abbey knew better than to pretend she didn't understand. "It was all right, I guess, for the first time. Frank and I are certainly not soulmates, but then I don't imagine you expected we would be. It'll take some time to be comfortable, for both of us." Her little speech sounded stiff, as if it had been prepared, which in fact it had. But it also, Abbey hoped, sounded like a loving daughter who would do her best to understand and cooperate if only she wasn't pushed.

Janice sat down on the edge of the bed. "Abbey, I know you think I'm hurrying things..."

"There's no need to be in a rush, that's for sure." Abbey twisted her pillows to a more comfortable angle. "Where does Frank live these days?"

"He still manages the apartment complex across the park, so he has one of the units."

Abbey nodded. "Did he park his truck somewhere else tonight?"

"No, he walked over. Why?"

"Just to be discreet?"

"I didn't ask him to, Abbey, if that's what you're implying. I suppose he may have thought you would be more comfortable if the occasion wasn't made public."

Abbey winced a little at the sharp edge in her mother's voice. "Mom, I just want you to be sure. Give yourself a chance to think it over, that's all."

"Abbey, believe me, I know exactly what I'm doing." Janice's tone was firm. "Wayne didn't call?"

Abbey shook her head. "I did notice one thing tonight," she said with an air of innocence. "Frank isn't the least bit acquisitive about the house, is he?"

Janice seemed to be relieved at the lack of sarcasm in the question. "Of course not."

"He didn't even seem interested." Abbey sneaked a glance at her mother. "Though I'm not surprised, really. How could he be comfortable around all the reminders of Daddy?"

"I think it's more likely that over the years he's seen every creaking board and cracked pipe and missing shingle," Janice said wryly. "That tends to take the romance out of an old house in a hurry. That, and the difficulty in getting help."

Abbey frowned, momentarily distracted. "Norma isn't seriously ill, is she?"

"No, but she's well past sixty and feeling a bit tired." Janice stood up. "I'm having breakfast with Wayne tomorrow, so I probably won't see you till lunchtime."

Abbey stretched. "I may just take a sandwich over to the library so I can work all day." She turned out the light when her mother left and lay staring half-amused at the bars of moonlight that crept across the carpet. So her mother was going off to plot strategy with Wayne again, was she?

That's one for me, Abbey thought. Janice hadn't expected this reaction from her daughter, and it had thrown her off her stride.

Unless... It was awfully funny how Wayne Marshall's name kept coming up, even at moments of stress when he should have been the last thing on Janice's mind. She'd even jumped directly from defending her feelings for Frank to asking if Wayne had called while she was out.

She was changing the subject, Abbey reminded herself with a yawn. And yet...what a strange way to choose to do it. Almost Freudian in its implications....

Dim suspicion tugged at the corners of Abbey's mind, but she lost hold of the thought as she slid into sleep. It couldn't possibly be anything but wishful thinking to suspect that Wayne, not Frank, might actually be the one who was constantly on Janice's mind these days.

ABBEY WASN'T SURPRISED when Frank accepted without comment the way she had organized the symphony concert and the party following. He might not even realize there was something faintly off-color about meeting Janice at the concert hall rather than picking her up at the house.

When Janice made no protest, Abbey found herself wondering what her mother could possibly be thinking. Janice was a stickler for manners; no boy Abbey ever dated had been spared parental inspection while he waited in the drawing room for Abbey to come downstairs. And though this situation was hardly the same as a couple of teenagers going out for pizza and a movie, Janice ought to have objected. But the only thing she said was a mild, "And how do you suggest we get to the concert, Abbey? Take a cab?"

Hastily Abbey offered her plan, and Janice meekly agreed to let Wayne Marshall and Boyd Baxter escort them.

What Abbey didn't say, but had been thinking all week, was that if they appeared with Wayne and Boyd in tow, running into the Grangers would look like an accident. She was relatively certain that Janice would work that out, too, and she had braced herself for an argument. The fact that she got not even half-smothered resistance left Abbey reeling, until she realized that her campaign must be having an effect already. She was actually succeeding in making Janice more sensitive to what her friends and neighbors would think of this idiotic engagement of hers. And if she could just keep up the pressure, surely Janice would soon see the light and call it off.

Abbey's timing was perfect to the minute; she was just pulling on the elbow-length black gloves that matched her slim and slinky long gown when the doorbell rang. She checked the diamond studs in her ears, smoothed a hand over her upswept hair, and dropped her lipstick in her tiny evening bag. She was coming slowly down the stairs—her narrow skirt didn't encourage anything faster—by the time Norma opened the front door.

Boyd Baxter stepped into the hallway and looked up. The expression on his face was all Abbey could have desired. His eyes widened, the pupils dilating in wonder, and he came to the foot of the stairs to offer his hand to help her down the last couple of steps.

"Thank you, Norma," Abbey said softly, without taking her eyes off Boyd. "I'll get the door next time."

"That's good," Norma said dryly. "All this back and forth stuff gets to me." She disappeared down the hallway, muttering to herself.

"Don't mind Norma," Abbey said to Boyd. "She's just cranky because of all the preparations for the party. She never has gotten along with caterers, but Mother insisted she have help this time."

"Who?" Boyd said. "Oh, you mean the maid. I didn't pay any attention."

Abbey smiled at him and wasted a moment in regret for her four-inch heels; she hadn't realized they would put her eyes on a level just a shade above Boyd's, and the added effect of her upswept hair probably made her look like an Amazon beside him.

The bell rang again, and she went to greet Wayne Marshall. He absentmindedly kissed the air beside her cheek. Abbey was about to tease him about that when she realized what had seized his attention. Janice was at the top of the stairs, poised with one hand on the polished banister. Her dress was severely plain, a straight sheath of pale gray silk. Nestled in the draped neckline was a heavy silver chain, and her earrings were small sterling blocks.

Suddenly Abbey found herself wondering if Janice had watched from the terrace for Wayne's car so she could time her entrance. If she had, the ploy certainly worked; Wayne raised a hand to tug at his bow tie, and Janice floated down the stairs to him. "You are by far the most beautiful woman I know," he said, and Janice smiled up at him with intimate warmth.

The depth of feeling in his voice made Abbey blink, and the vague suspicions that had been floating through her mind all week crystallized into absolute certainty.

It wasn't Frank Granger Janice wanted, after all. It was Wayne Marshall.

And now that both Janice and Wayne knew it, surely...

But there wasn't time to think it all out now. Boyd had picked up Abbey's shawl, a spider's web of black lace, and Wayne had already placed Janice's hand into the bend of his elbow. He was patting it, in fact.

Abbey found herself chewing her lower lip all the way down Armitage Road. She would have liked to glance over her shoulder to see if Janice and Wayne were holding hands in the back seat of Boyd's car, but she smothered the temptation. It was better right now not to know.

What in heaven's name was Janice going to do? As if the situation weren't already enough of a mess! This development could do nothing but make it worse—Frank would be terribly hurt.

At least they hadn't announced the engagement. That was one thing to be grateful for. And Janice certainly had enough class not to make a public fuss just because she had got a shock.

But in truth, Abbey reflected, Janice hadn't looked as if it were a shock to her at all. *Wayne* had seemed somewhat stunned, true, but Janice...

Was Janice capable of creating this entire scenario just so Wayne Marshall would realize how important she was to him? After all, he'd had six years, and he apparently hadn't offered Janice anything more than friendship. But if he were to see her slipping away... No, her mother couldn't be so cruel.

"What a frown," Janice whispered as they waited by the entrance for Boyd to park the car and return. "I've got aspirin if you've developed a headache, Abbey."

Abbey shot a sideways look at Wayne, still standing close to Janice. There was no chance to say anything to her mother now.

Inside, the noise was subsiding as the crowd was slowly ushered to seats in the big new auditorium. Frank was leaning against the lobby wall, waiting, his dark gray suit a sharp contrast to the pale bricks.

He was going to stand out in the crowd at Abbey's party, that was for sure. All the men in the Staffords' circle habitually wore tuxedos to the symphony, and she had assumed her mother would fill Frank in on what was expected, so she hadn't specified dress on the invitations. Now she felt a little ashamed of herself. Frank might, with some justification, think she'd intended to make him feel ill at ease.

Then again, it was quite likely Janice *had* told him and Frank simply refused to conform. If that was what had happened, no wonder Janice was looking at Wayne's faultless tuxedo with approval.

Keep it up, Abbey, she warned herself, *and you're going to need that aspirin!*

Beside Frank was a man in evening clothes and when he turned toward them, Abbey's breath caught in her throat. But at least she knew now that Frank was simply being contrary and she could stop worrying about his feelings—for here was Flynn, complete with pleated shirt and pearl studs, coming to greet them.

The seating arrangement worked itself out so casually that no one in the auditorium could have suspected it had been planned. Frank was on the aisle, with Janice next to him and Wayne at her other side; then came Boyd, and Abbey, with Flynn bringing up the rear. And since their seats were nearly at the front of the big auditorium, they occupied the entire row of the center section.

Abbey let Boyd fuss with her shawl and program, but when his attention was distracted by a woman in the row ahead of them, Flynn murmured almost in her ear, "You're being awfully quiet."

"I'm stunned." She let her fingertips brush against his coat sleeve. "At our high-school awards night, if there had been a category for 'Most Likely Never to Wear Evening Clothes,' you'd have won it hands down, Flynn."

He shrugged. "I thought you'd expect it. If I'd had any idea I could get away without making a monkey of myself..."

"Where did you get it?"

"There's a place downtown that rents them," Flynn said airily.

"Right." Abbey's voice was dry. "Aren't you lucky they could manage a perfect fit?" Did he think she was an idiot, not to recognize good tailoring? That tuxedo hadn't come off any rack.

The house lights died just then, and in the rustle as the audience settled down, Flynn said, "Well, at least I'm wearing it with dignity. Boyd looks like a simpleton. Or does that foolish smirk of his have something to do with you?"

Abbey would have cheerfully ground her spike heel into his foot, but he sensed her movement and dodged just in time.

"I'll bet that's it," he murmured. "Those high heels of yours were a very bad choice, you know. They make him look inconsequential."

She couldn't help muttering, "I would have sworn he was taller than that."

"He hasn't shrunk. You were running around in your socks that night he stopped by. Don't you remember? I was astounded you'd forgotten yourself like that."

The conductor appeared and raised his baton. To Abbey's relief, and Flynn's credit, Flynn seemed familiar with proper concert etiquette, and he didn't breathe another word all the way through the Rachmaninoff piano concerto. He didn't applaud in the wrong places, either.

Abbey didn't hear much of the music. She was too busy thinking through all the disjointed bits of information she'd been picking up all week, and by the time intermission approached she could barely contain herself. "I have to talk to you," she hissed to Flynn even before the last emphatic notes of the concerto died away.

"Shush," said a woman in the row behind them.

Flynn only raised an eyebrow. Under cover of the applause, he slid from his seat and held out a hand. By the time Boyd realized Abbey had moved, they were halfway down the aisle. "At least we've managed to wipe the silly smile off his face," Flynn said.

But Abbey's narrow skirt slowed their progress, and when they reached the lobby, they were surrounded by people. When Flynn stopped there, she shook her head. "Privately."

"This isn't about Boyd, is it? Because if you brought me here to tell me you were out with him last night, I already know."

Abbey stopped short. "Why do you think it would be any possible business of yours if I date Boyd?"

"Oh, it isn't, unless you've told him about your scheme." He pushed wide the side doors of the building, which opened onto the parklike commons of the campus.

"Of course I haven't. That whole business about the fund-raising committee could have been a cover-up, you know. Didn't you even see that?"

"A cover-up? With Boyd in on it? Don't make me laugh."

The commons was complete with winding paths and big old trees and geometric flower gardens. Flynn hurried her along, and by the time they reached a private corner at the far side of the grassy area, in the shadow of an ancient Scotch pine tree, Abbey was short of breath.

Abbey clutched her chest and managed, "Your father seems to be enjoying the concert."

"That's the little observation for which you needed privacy?"

"No, I was just commenting."

"There's your answer to what to give them for a wedding present. Symphony tickets. On the other hand, with *Bolero* coming up, he might even fulfill your expectations by falling asleep."

"That is not—"

"Of course, any respecer of music would be capable of that. Now, what was it you wanted to tell me?"

She wanted to put her nose in the air and go back to the auditorium, but conscience made her stay. "I think you should warn your father, Flynn."

"Why?"

Abbey took a deep breath. "Because I think Mother is only using him to make someone else notice she's available and attractive."

His eyebrows soared. "Why?"

"Can't you say anything but 'why?' Never mind. Because it's someone who ought to have noticed her long ago and didn't."

"That's . . ."

They were standing close together on the path, their voices low. Abbey was trying to see the expression in his eyes, but the shadows were too deep to tell if he was taking her seriously. She took a breath in order to try again, at the exact moment Flynn's arm went around her. "What the—" she managed to say in the half second before her body collided with his and the air was jolted out of her lungs.

"Just shut up and play along," he hissed in her ear.

There certainly wasn't much else she could do. She was pressed so tightly against him she couldn't even get enough leverage to kick; his hold was like a trap, and her arms were pinned so she couldn't slap him, either. His other hand moved up to cup the side of her face and turn it to his, and his mouth brushed hers softly, then settled into a demanding kiss.

Play along? What on earth was the man up to? But she didn't have much choice. The only parts of her that were still free to move were her hands and wrists, and their range was limited.

Flynn's fingertips teased the soft tendrils of loose hair at her temple, and the tip of his tongue traced the line of her lips for a moment. *Play along,* Abbey reminded herself hazily, and relaxed against him.

The action seemed to take him by surprise, because he tensed for just a second before giving a low, breathless laugh. And the next kiss was demanding in an entirely different way—it was sultry and possessive and persuasive, and it went on nearly forever.

When finally Flynn let her go, Abbey staggered and would have stepped back into the sharp needles of the Scotch pine if he hadn't grabbed her arm again and pulled her onto the path.

"Are you all right?" he asked. But the carefully solicitous tone was tinged with laughter.

Abbey growled, "Would you mind telling me what the hell you thought you were doing?"

Flynn shrugged. "It started out to be a kiss." He shook his head a little, as if he were trying to clear it. "Thanks for the cooperation. You went above and beyond the call of duty, I'd say.''

''What duty? Will you tell me what's going on?''

''Somebody was coming along the path. I didn't think we should be caught in that discussion, so—''

''So instead, you made it look like a seduction in progress?'' She stamped her foot. ''Dammit, Flynn!''

''Well, nobody in a crowd like this is going to stop and stare at an embracing couple. It's impolite. Besides, all men in evening clothes look alike, that dress of yours melts into the shadows, and I think I had your face covered with my hand. Nobody will know who we were.''

She released a long, infuriated groan. ''Well, before anyone else comes along, can we finish our talk?''

''Nobody else will be coming. Intermission is over.'' He tugged at her hand. ''And if we're not back soon, Boyd will call out the law to search for us.''

He wasn't far wrong. The conductor was just stepping onto the podium when Abbey slid breathlessly into her seat. Boyd held up his program and hissed behind it, ''I almost came looking for you.''

She pantomimed frustration and sank into her seat, waving her own program distractedly in order to cool her hot cheeks.

As the first plaintive bassoon wailed the theme of *Bolero,* Flynn murmured, ''What do you see in him, anyway, besides a receding hairline?''

Abbey gave him a look that would have melted an ordinary man into a whimpering puddle.

Flynn, of course, only laughed.

CHAPTER FIVE

MIDWAY THROUGH the second half of the concert, Flynn propped his elbow on the armrest they shared, put his cheek against his fist and to all appearances dropped off to sleep. If Abbey had had a pin, she'd have poked him. As it was, she kept expecting him to begin snoring, and so she didn't enjoy a minute of the music herself. And with Boyd, Wayne and her mother in the way, she couldn't even get the satisfaction of looking down the row to see whether Frank Granger was doing the same thing.

Afterward, there wasn't a chance for a private word with anyone in the crush of greetings as the crowd made its way to the parking lot. And for the first half hour of her party at the Stafford house, Abbey didn't even catch a glimpse of Flynn. He hadn't just gone home to bed, had he? *Had he?*

She definitely had a headache now, and she couldn't wait for the party to be over. Why had she ever thought this evening would prove anything? More to the point, why hadn't she seen through her mother long ago? At the moment, Janice was in the morning room with most of the members of her bridge club gathered around, and Frank—well, who knew where Frank was? Abbey had seen him earlier going into the library. By now he might be halfway through a book. Or, if he were completely

bored with the party, he might even be out trimming the
dead oak tree.

Maybe she should hunt him down and warn him herself, since Flynn apparently wasn't interested enough to
take care of it. But Abbey quailed at the thought of facing Frank directly.

Most of the guests had drinks in hand and were sampling the caterer's bounty before Abbey felt free to slip
away and track down Flynn. In the drawing room, Boyd
was toying with the piano; he waved her over, but Abbey
shook her head and continued her search. Sara Merrill,
the young professor who had been such a help with the
Elizabethan papers, caught Abbey's eye and, pitching her
voice so as not to interfere with the heated exchange going on around her, said, "Looking for Flynn?" Without
waiting for an answer, she pointed casually toward the
terrace and turned back to the argument.

Abbey gulped. If her intentions were so obvious to
Sara Merrill, she'd better be more careful, or other people would be picking up vibrations, too. Still, she was
grateful for the assistance. Flynn was perched on the
stone rail of the terrace in the dimmest, most out-of-the-
way corner; she could have missed him altogether. Half
a dozen others had sought the peaceful fresh air, but they
were in a clump near the door, and Abbey easily moved
past, able to decline their invitation to join them because of her duties as hostess.

Flynn was sitting sideways on the rail, one foot drawn
up and his hands folded on his knee as he looked out
across the garden. There was no impatience in his pose;
he might have been sitting there for thirty seconds or
forever.

Two tulip glasses of champagne stood on the rail beside him, bubbles hanging in the golden liquid. He shifted

when he saw her and held out a glass. "I thought you'd be along," he murmured.

"If I'd known where you were, I wouldn't have kept you waiting so long." Her voice was mock apologetic.

"Don't worry about it. I was just thinking."

"Heaven forbid."

"Maybe I've been wrong about you all along," Flynn said pensively. "You certainly don't kiss like a prim and proper Armitage Road girl."

Just the mention of that kiss made her feel a little light-headed. But she kept her voice level. "Who are you comparing me to? Your landlady?"

He raised his glass with a smile, but instead of answering, he said, "I thought you told me this would be a small party."

"As parties on Armitage Road go, it is. Not that it was worth the effort."

"Oh? Do you mean this brainstorm you've had about your mother's Machiavellian plans? Have you told Frank yet?"

"No, I thought that should be your job."

"Why would she pick on him, anyway?"

"I don't know. Frank must have realized all along, subconsciously, at least, how ridiculous this engagement is. So I can only suppose she thinks he won't be hurt when she eventually breaks it off and announces she's really interested in Wayne."

Flynn choked on his champagne, and Abbey ended up pounding him on the back till he could breathe again. "Abbey," he finally managed, "Wayne Marshall is gay!"

She looked at him suspiciously over the edge of her glass. "How do you know?"

He looked amused. "Well, not from firsthand experience, I assure you. But believe me, I know."

Abbey released a long, exasperated breath. "Wayne's where she's getting all her guidance and support in her choice! Well, that's crazy! What kind of marital advice can he give?"

Flynn eyed her cautiously. "But a minute ago you said... Never mind. Abbey, the blinding speed of your changing attitudes overwhelms me."

"I'm stunned."

"That's apparent. You might want to keep your voice down."

"Why? Everybody's gone." She frowned and looked around the terrace, suddenly uneasy. "Wait a minute. Why did everybody disappear?"

Now that she stopped to think about it, she had a vague recollection of someone inside the house calling for attention, asking the crowd to be quiet. But she hadn't really paid much notice; she'd been too busy with Flynn's coughing fit.

Flynn slid off the terrace rail and lifted her down. "I think we'd better find out."

The crowd had gathered in the long hallway. Despite the size and length of the hall, not everyone could fit, and the crush was such that Abbey couldn't see over the heads of the people who blocked the arched doorway of the drawing room.

She worked her way into the fringes of the group until she could reach out and tug at Boyd's sleeve. "What's going on?" she demanded.

His jaw was tight. "You ought to know," he said coolly. "Your mother and Frank Granger are announcing an engagement, that's what."

Eyes wide with shock, Abbey wriggled back through the crowd to Flynn's side, grabbed his arm with both hands and yanked it. "You have to stop them," she hissed. "They can't do this!"

He shook his head. He was looking over the crowd, and his eyes were narrowed. "I warned you this couldn't be kept under wraps forever, Abbey."

"But Mother promised she wouldn't announce it!"

"Are you certain of that?"

Abbey stood on tiptoe, but even then she couldn't see much. She got a glimpse of Janice halfway up the staircase, and she thought she saw Frank standing beside her. But there was no doubt about what she was hearing: Janice was inviting everyone to the wedding.

"Do you still think I should tell him she isn't serious?" Flynn muttered.

Abbey's head was spinning—Janice *had* promised to keep the news under wraps, hadn't she?—and it took a full minute for her to realize that the murmurs she was hearing from the people around her did not reflect polite surprise, but confusion. Startled, she glanced up at Flynn. No, the reaction wasn't her imagination; her concern was mirrored in his eyes.

"It's not much comfort to have my judgment confirmed," she muttered back. She wasn't heartless; she could certainly feel the hurt that must be sweeping over Janice and Frank right now at the reaction their joyful announcement engendered.

Flynn shook his head. "Don't you see? They expected it was us."

She gave a hoot of half-hysterical laughter. "What?"

He looked grim. "Somebody obviously recognized us at intermission, after all. There've been whispers all during the party—didn't you hear them?"

"I had more important things to do." Then for the first time she really took in what he had said. "You mean..."

"Everybody expected the announcement to be *our* engagement, not your mother's and my father's. No wonder they're confused."

"You and your bright ideas," Abbey said gloomily. "All men look alike in evening clothes, my foot! You stand out a mile!"

Sara Merrill tapped her on the shoulders. "I hate to intrude, but in the interests of fairness, it wasn't Flynn's tuxedo that gave you away," she confided helpfully. "It was the gloves. You're the only woman in town who was wearing gloves tonight. Everybody noticed, so when you got into that clinch on the path, and Flynn, like a gentleman, turned his back to the public to conceal the identity of the lady in his arms..."

Abbey remembered the way she had clutched at him, and groaned. "A lot you know about this crowd, Flynn Granger. They're too polite to stare at an embracing couple, I think you said. Ha!"

Flynn said irritably, "Was everybody in the damned auditorium out for a walk tonight?"

The guests began to disperse again, heading back to the buffet table or forming new groups to talk over this startling tidbit. In the drawing room, someone turned on the stereo system, and several couples drifted out to the terrace to dance.

Boyd came over to Abbey, grinning sheepishly. "I was afraid there for a minute that Janice would be talking about you. Guess I should have known better, shouldn't I?"

"You certainly—" Abbey began.

Flynn took her arm firmly. "I think we'd better go and congratulate our parents, don't you?"

Abbey drew herself up to protest, but the expression in his eyes quelled any answer at all.

Once they were away from Boyd, Flynn said under his breath, "Or we will risk increasing the level of talk about how strange this whole affair is. At least they didn't drag us up on center stage earlier. A wise move of course—you couldn't have kept your outrage to yourself.... What *do* you see in him, anyway?"

"You mean Boyd?" She pulled away. "Boyd's sweet. He saw me at the Talbots' party and immediately wanted to get to know me."

Flynn snorted. "Immediately? Is that why he waited another forty-eight hours till he was sure you were suitable, as well as pretty? He must have been tickled when he found out you were Warren Stafford's daughter, since it makes you a double prize."

Abbey sniffed. "And what would you do if you saw someone you were attracted to at a party? March straight up to her, I suppose, and say, 'Hi, do you want to get acquainted? I'd like you to be a significant person in my life.'"

"Something like that," Flynn murmured as they reached Janice and Frank. He smiled at Janice and kissed her cheek. "May I start calling you Mom now, or must I wait till after the wedding?"

Janice gave him a soft smile. "Oh, Flynn, I'd love to have you call me that."

Abbey could understand why her mother was enchanted; the scamp could charm the birds from the trees. Abbey, though, found his easy allure a bit disgusting. She tried to ignore the exchange and turned to the man standing beside her mother. It would be just as well to make it clear right now that no matter what Flynn said or did, Frank was not going to be "Dad" to her.

"Best wishes, Frank," she said, extending both hands to him. She did not offer her cheek for a kiss, and she was glad he made no effort to bridge the distance between them.

"I know this isn't easy for you, Abbey." His pale blue eyes were serious, and his grip was firm. "I want you to know that your mother is very important to me."

Abbey's gaze dropped. She was relieved she hadn't made a fool of herself by telling him her speculations about Janice and Wayne.

"The last weekend of June," she heard Janice say to a woman she was hugging. "It won't be an elaborate wedding of course, but there are so many people..."

Abbey's heart sank. It was the end of May now, so Janice had less than a month to come to her senses. And now that she had compounded the problem by bringing the whole town in on it, would she be more likely to see how foolish she had been? Or would her pride make it even harder for her to admit her mistake?

But there was nothing for Abbey to do but finish out her party, smiling and making the best of it even when she was congratulated for the smooth surprise she had managed to pull off. "Who'd have thought this would turn out to be an engagement party?" one matron commented.

Who indeed, Abbey thought. Certainly not the hostess.

Then the matron added with a naughty chuckle, "At least for that particular pair. I think everybody had it wrong. Yes, quite a bombshell, Abbey. Is that the only one, or do you have another shocker up your sleeve?"

That did it for Abbey. She decided to never speak to Flynn Granger again, or look at him, or come within half a mile of the man. Surely then the gossip would die down....

"In about half a million years," she muttered. "If I'm lucky."

"What was that, Abbey?" Wayne Marshall asked. "Have you taken up geology or something?"

She glared at him.

"Well, never mind," he said hastily. "I'm glad you're being such a good sport about this. It's your mother's life, after all, and her decision."

"And something tells me it was her good friend Wayne who advised her to spring the announcement on us tonight. Am I right?"

He looked a little uneasy.

"Don't bother to deny it. Wayne, how could you encourage her to embarrass herself in public like this?"

"Abbey, your mother did not raise you to be this sort of snob."

"I am not a snob! If I thought for one minute she'd be happy, I wouldn't mind if she married Tarzan!"

"Well, you might stop treating Frank like an ape."

"I don't have anything against Frank personally. It's just that they're all wrong together. Can't anyone but me see that? If she was marrying you, I'd be delighted." Then honesty forced her to modify the statement. "Well, at least I wouldn't be afraid for her."

"Abbey," Wayne said awkwardly, "I'm not looking for a wife."

Abbey sighed. "I know, and that's not the point. But if I came home with a completely unsuitable man, my mother would have a fit—and you'd support her then, too, I suppose."

Wayne shook his head. "Even if your mother didn't like your choice, she would accept him because of her love for you."

"I hope that if my mother thought I was making the worst mistake of my life, she would kick and scream and try to change my mind."

"Every person has a right to make her own mistakes, Abbey."

"Good," Abbey said sweetly. "I'm glad you're at least admitting the possibility that my mother is making a big one." She moved off to say good-night to the first departing guests, and this time when Boyd caught her eye, she promptly joined him.

For the rest of the evening, she stayed on the watch for Flynn so she could avoid him. But he seemed to have read her mind, for he made himself scarce. In fact, she didn't catch a glimpse of him again until the last of the guests had gone, and then he showed up in the kitchen, where Abbey was supervising the cleanup.

He eyed the catering staff and lowered his voice. "How about having breakfast with me tomorrow?"

Abbey shook her head. "I'm sleeping as late as possible and then going to brunch at the country club with Boyd."

Flynn whistled admiringly. "That should thoroughly confuse the gossips."

"Somebody's got to do something to correct the impression you left with them tonight."

"The impression *I* left?" He shook his head sadly. "As if you didn't help."

"If I'd known what I was letting myself in for, I certainly would have stayed in my seat during intermission. And I'm not interested in adding to the problem by being seen with you again, either."

"Don't you think it will look even more suspicious if we studiously avoid each other? We're going to be related, you know—if only in a roundabout sort of way."

Abbey bristled. "I haven't resigned myself to that yet. Have you?"

"Not exactly. But I think we can safely say your plan was a flop. Let me know whenever you're interested in hearing about mine."

SLEEPING LATE HAD BEEN a lovely, inviting idea, but it was still relatively early when Abbey found herself pushing back the blankets, too restless to stay in bed. Instead, she curled up on the wide seat in front of the casement window in her bedroom. She saw Norma leave the house on her way to church, and she watched as Janice came down the steps from the screened-in porch at the back of the house and wandered through the garden.

She felt a little guilty spying on her mother, but even from a distance, Abbey could see that this walk was not Janice's usual purposeful survey of the trees and flowers. She was moving aimlessly along the paths, and her shoulders sagged as if she was tired.

She ought to be happy, Abbey thought. *I know I'm the one preventing that. But I wonder if there's something else, as well.*

Last night, by the time everyone had left the party, it had been too late for a heart-to-heart chat. Besides, Abbey admitted, she hadn't felt like discussing anything at all with her mother right then. She'd been afraid that in their mutual exhaustion, if they once started to lose control, all sorts of accusations and charges might spill out. Things like that left lasting scars.

But they were going to have to talk sometime, that was certain. So Abbey pulled on a pair of khaki shorts and a pink T-shirt and went to join her mother.

Janice was bending over a bed of irises, which were just starting to show deep purple along the swollen buds. She looked up with a tentative smile. "Hello, darling. Did you sleep well?"

"Not particularly." Abbey sat down on the brick wall bordering the flower bed. It was low, and her feet sprawled out into the path. She stared at the toes of her pink canvas shoes. "I thought you weren't going to make an announcement just yet."

Janice sighed. "It was rude of me to use your party. I'm sorry."

Abbey pounced. "But you're not sorry you made the announcement?"

"I'm not sorry I didn't wait for your permission, that's true." Janice plucked a weed out of the flower bed and, dusting off her hands, turned to look Abbey straight in the eye. "And I never promised I *would* wait, my dear."

She was probably correct about that, Abbey thought. Janice had simply remained quiet about the whole thing, and Abbey had made the foolish assumption that her silence meant agreement. "I wasn't implying that you need my permission, Mother. I just asked for some time."

"How much time did you want?" Janice asked. "Weeks? Months? Years?"

Abbey felt a guilty flush creeping into her face. "More than than the few days you gave me," she said stubbornly.

Janice turned back to her weeding. "I didn't think it was likely to make any difference, no matter how long we waited. If I was wrong about that, I'm sorry."

Abbey jumped up from the wall. "If I could only understand what you see in him, Mother, it might help. But I honestly don't comprehend how you could choose someone like Frank after being married to Daddy!"

Janice's eyes were sad and her voice was soft. "If you really want to understand, Abbey, it won't take any explanation from me. You're a smart girl—you can look at Frank and see. And if you don't honestly want to understand, an explanation won't do any good."

Abbey released a long breath of frustration. "But he hardly ever says a word! I'd just like to know how you ever got to know him well enough to think you want to spend the rest of your life with him. That would satisfy me for the moment."

Janice's forehead wrinkled. "I suppose I first realized how much he meant to me when he was trying to fix the wobbly leg on the dining-room table and the whole thing came down on top of him."

Abbey studied her mother and said nothing.

"It's a heavy table. I thought for a minute it had killed him, and...well, that's when I knew. At any rate, as long as we're talking about furniture, is there anything in the house you're particularly attached to, Abbey? Things that you'll want someday, even though you don't have a place for them now?"

"You sound as if you're disposing of your estate."

Janice smiled a little. "I suppose I am, in a sense. If you'll make a list, I'll have the moving company pack the things up and put them in storage."

"What's wrong with leaving them right where they are?"

"That's not possible." Janice took a deep breath, as if bracing herself. "I'm going to sell the house, Abbey."

BOYD APPEARED to be just as shocked as Abbey felt, when she gave him the news over Belgian waffles at the country club.

"I didn't know she had that in mind," he mused. "Of course, she has every right to sell the house, unless your father mentioned you in his will in connection with the property."

"No," Abbey said impatiently. "There's some money and stock in trust for me, but the house belongs to Mother. It's not the fact she's selling it that bothers me, anyway. What in heaven's name would I do with it? I'm certainly not going to live here."

"You wouldn't even consider it? But Abbey—"

Abbey ignored the interruption. "It's the idea of my mother giving up her lovely home to live in the caretaker's apartment in a complex on the wrong side of the park. And then she had the nerve to tell me she was amazed at my surprise, since I'd practically suggested it myself."

Boyd frowned. "I don't see—"

"What I said was that Frank couldn't be very comfortable surrounded by my father's things. I hoped it would make her think about the contrast between them. I had no idea she'd decide to give it all up for a fresh start!"

"I can certainly see your point. Warren's books and art pieces would make someone nervous if he didn't understand and appreciate them."

Abbey wasn't listening. "If you can call it a fresh start, that is. Those apartments must be thirty years old, and the way tenants move in and out I'm amazed they're still standing." She stared at the bite of waffle on her fork as if wondering what it was, then put it down. She had no appetite left.

"Well, the house is awfully big," Boyd said judiciously. "And with your housekeeper retiring..."

Abbey blinked in surprise. "Norma's retiring? That's the first I've heard of it."

Boyd flushed. "I shouldn't have brought it up, I suppose."

"Why not?"

"Because it's legal business. Your mother came in to arrange a pension for her. So I'd appreciate it if you wouldn't say I'm the one who let it slip. Still, I'm surprised Janice didn't tell me then that she was thinking of selling the house."

"I'm not surprised," Abbey said grimly. "You've heard the expression about waiting for the other shoe to drop? Well, I'm beginning to think my mother's a centipede. Damn, here comes trouble."

Boyd glanced over his shoulder. "Who—"

"Mrs. Austin, in the flesh. You mean you haven't met her? Well, watch out. She's the worst busybody in town."

"That tiny little lady? But she looks so frail."

"Appearances can be deceiving," Abbey said darkly.

Mrs. Austin leaned on an ebony cane as she made her way purposefully across the dining room to their table. Boyd jumped to his feet and discarded his napkin just as she arrived, and she rewarded him with an approving smile and a pat on the arm. "It's so nice to see a young man with proper manners," she murmured. "My congratulations, Abbey, for recognizing the important things. I am told that your mother had some interesting news last night. Is it true she's going to be married again?"

"Oh, yes. Quite true."

"Hmm. You don't look excited, somehow."

Abbey managed to smile. "I'm thrilled. If it makes my mother happy—"

"Frank Granger?" Mrs. Austin said with a delicate touch of scorn. "It must be infatuation. Unless... I wonder how long it's been since Janice has had a thorough medical checkup." She tipped her head back to stare at Abbey through half-hooded eyes.

The woman looked extraordinarily like a well-fed vulture, Abbey thought.

"That must be it," Mrs. Austin said wisely. "You might encourage her to see a specialist, Abbey. Things do happen, you know, as we get older. It would be unfortunate to find out too late that Janice was suffering from hardening of the arteries and not love at all. Frank Granger," she said once more almost to herself, and shook her head sadly as she returned to her own table.

"'Things do happen as we get older,'" Abbey repeated with a sniff. "She ought to know, the witch. Still, that's the final straw. Wouldn't you think Mother would mind that half the town believes she's got a case of early senility? What in heaven's name is she thinking of?"

Boyd looked worried. "You don't suppose she's right? Mrs. Austin, I mean. If Janice did have one of those awful diseases that slowly robs the brain of oxygen..."

"Oh, please. You serve on a committee with her, Boyd. Don't you think you'd have noticed if her mental state was beginning to slip?"

"It would explain everything," Boyd said stubbornly. "I mean, Frank Granger... It does make one wonder about Janice's judgment."

Abbey bit her tongue. It was hardly fair to be irritated at Boyd for coming up with the same questions she herself had asked Janice not three hours ago. Still, he didn't need to make Frank sound as if he had leprosy, or didn't know a fork from a pocketknife, or had never worn shoes!

She shook her head, confused by her own reaction, and then realized that she'd seen a similar thing happen in big families, where siblings fought continually but joined forces if threatened from outside.

This whole schizophrenic feeling I've got is family loyalty, she mused. *If anybody's going to attack my mother, it's going to be me!*

A half hour later Boyd walked her to the front door of the house. Politeness decreed she should ask him in for coffee, but Abbey was impatient to be free so she could try again to reach Flynn. He hadn't been answering his telephone earlier, and Abbey was anxious to find out what his plan was now that Janice had dropped the news about the house. It was apparent someone was going to have to do something, and fast.

Before she had made up her mind, Boyd stopped on the terrace. "I'd love to come in, Abbey, but I've got a load of paperwork I have to finish this afternoon. Perhaps I can see you later in the week?"

She agreed and went inside, trying to think up an excuse to change her clothes and immediately escape from the house again. But the rooms were ominously silent, and on the kitchen table she found a note from Janice. She and Frank had gone for a drive to put flowers on the family plots in the old cemeteries nearby. Obviously they wouldn't be back for hours.

"What a perfect family outing," Abbey muttered. "Too bad I'm missing it."

She picked up a notepad and pencil on her way out the door; if Flynn still weren't at home, she could at least leave him a message. The windows of the chauffeur's quarters above Flora Pembroke's garage stood open to the May sunshine when Abbey arrived and when she climbed the old stone stairs and tapped on the screen door, Flynn called out an order to come in.

After the brilliant sunshine, the rooms seemed dim and dark, and Abbey stood just inside the door and blinked a few times. In the far corner by the biggest window, Flynn leaned around his easel and said impatiently, "The place isn't going to give you typhoid, you know. It may not be stylish, but it's perfectly clean."

Her eyes had adjusted by then, and she could see that he was absolutely correct. The windows were bare and no two pieces of furniture were the same style, much less a matched set, but somehow the total effect wasn't forlorn but inviting. In fact, the room had the charm of a little stone cottage, with its angled walls and slanted ceilings. Of course, Abbey thought as she moved into the room, it cried out for curtains—something crisp and simple— and bright rag rugs and chintz slipcovers, but she could almost forget that it was above a garage.

She glanced over his shoulder at the landscape he was working on.

She was silent so long that finally Flynn put his brush down and turned to look at her. "What's got your tongue?"

"I didn't want to break your concentration."

"Stop staring, then."

"It won't bother you if I talk?" She nodded at the easel. "That's too wonderful for me to take a chance on ruining it."

"Sometimes it bothers me. Not at this stage." He picked up the brush again. Something about the way he held it, his long fingers firm on the smooth handle, made Abbey think of the way he had held her the night before on the path outside the auditorium, one hand against her face.

That was a performance, she reminded herself. Nevertheless, painting was obviously a sensual experience for him.

She curled up in a wing chair near the easel so she could watch as he worked. The chair's velvet covering, once probably maroon, was now a faded brownish pink, and was surprisingly comfortable. It sagged in all the right places. She draped one leg over the chair arm, nestled her cheek into the back and told him about the house.

"I suppose next she'll be growing her own vegetables," Abbey finished. "All in the interests of the simple life." She let her foot swing idly. "You're not surprised, are you?"

Flynn didn't look up from the landscape. "No. Not that I knew about the plan to sell the house, but it seems logical."

"Not to me."

"So maybe you can convince her to give the place to you."

"Why would *I* want it? It's too much for me to handle, even if I was going to live here."

"In that case, don't you understand why your mother might feel overwhelmed by the responsibility?"

Abbey shrugged. "Why should it be too much for her? She's going to have a full-time handyman." She sat up. "I think it's time to put your plan into operation. What is it, anyway?"

Flynn added a dark blue shadow to the side of a tree and said, "It's quite simple, really. You've been attacking the problem directly, while I approached it from a different angle."

"Using psychology, you mean?"

"Exactly." He took a step back and eyed the painting. "I'm not going to say a word about them. I won't even suggest they call off the wedding, but the net effect will be the same."

"Sounds like magic." She leaned back into the velvet upholstery and yawned.

"Oh, it is." He swirled his brush across the palette again and braced his elbow against the easel. "It's so perfectly simple it's elegant, Abbey. All we have to do is start having a flaming and very public affair."

CHAPTER SIX

ABBEY'S FOOT STOPPED in midswing. "You've got to be—" Her voice was no more than a panicky squeak. She gulped and cleared her throat several times, and when she managed to speak again, she sounded a little more like herself. "Have an affair? Us?"

"Who else did you think I was talking about?"

"I don't like the sound of this. Why you think it would solve anything if we—" Her voice failed again.

Flynn studied the painting again. "Because your mother will blame me for taking advantage of her sainted darling, and my father will blame you for—"

"Gold digging, I suppose?"

Flynn shot her a disgusted look. "Distracting me from my muse. Or making me too shaky to paint anything but blades of grass." He demonstrated, letting a theatrical tremor in his hand flick the brush against a scrap of paper to create a random pattern of lines. Tipping his head to one side, he studied the result and nodded. "I'd say that's more likely, when I think about it. Dad doesn't worry much about my muse, but he hates paintings that are nothing but grass. He says it shows a basic lack of creative energy."

Abbey wasn't listening. "Blaming each other's kid isn't going to make either of them think twice about getting married."

"Of course it will. They'll eventually transfer the blame to each other. Can't you see it, each of them accusing the other of raising a brat? The fallout will be so heavy they'll break up for sure."

"Because each of them will prefer solitude over having to claim us both?" Abbey rolled her eyes. "That's a pretty different angle, all right. I'm amazed you thought it up all by yourself."

"It was the reaction from the people at your party last night that gave me the idea," Flynn said modestly. "They all seemed to expect it, you see. It's not only a good plan, but half the work is already done."

Abbey found herself frowning as the disquieting image of Flynn's kissing her flashed in her mind. This whole conversation was growing so ridiculous she could hardly believe that for a moment she had almost taken him seriously.

Her foot start to swing again. "Well, if everyone in town anticipates—how did you put it, a flaming and very public affair?—then why do you think Frank and Mother would be shocked enough to break their engagement? They're likely to tell all their friends we're old enough to be responsible for ourselves and just not invite either of us home for Christmas."

There was something wrong with this talk—something uncomfortable. She shifted uneasily in the chair, and the toe of her sandal brushed Flynn's arm.

He jumped and swore. "Watch it! I'm not doing abstract art here, you know. If you put a black streak across my almost finished sunset, I'll tattoo a mustache on you."

Abbey snapped her fingers. "Now *that* would destroy your image with my mother, and more effectively than an affair would, I'd bet. Not that it matters. I'm not interested."

"In the mustache? Oh, you mean the affair." Flynn put down his brush and turned to look at her, arms folded across his chest. "I didn't criticize *your* plan."

"You most certainly did."

"All right, maybe I made a few suggestions for improving it. But even though you ignored my help, I didn't refuse to take part. I played my role to the best of my ability. And now when I ask you for moral support in return—"

"*Immoral* support, don't you mean? Flynn, your role in my plan consisted of holding down a seat at the symphony concert and being as charming as you could manage at my party. That is hardly the sort of wholehearted commitment you're asking of me. An affair, for heaven's sake—what are you thinking of?"

"I didn't say it had to be a real affair."

"Thank you," Abbey said with all the dignity she could muster. "But I had already assumed that a public performance was the outside limit of what you were requesting."

"Though if having a real affair would be easier for you than playing the part, I could be persuaded to go along, I suppose."

Abbey considered picking up the tray of paints and dumping it over his head. The idea of turning him into a rainbow would be appropriate, she thought. He was just as changeable and just as hard to grasp.

"No, thank you," she said with only a hint of sarcasm. "I mean, I realize what a generous offer you're making—"

"Don't mention it. There wouldn't be any real effort on my part."

Abbey went on ruthlessly. "And I'm quite aware of what an honor it would be to have my name linked with yours in gossip for all time, but I believe I'll take a rain check."

Flynn didn't seem disturbed. "Well, you think it over and let me know."

He released the painting from the easel and set it flat on a table at the far end of the big living room to finish drying. When he came back toward her, he didn't reach for another sheet of paper, as Abbey half expected he would; instead, he stood over her chair, hands on hips and looked at her.

She eyed him warily. "Am I developing a wart on the end of my nose or something?"

"Not at all. Humor me for a minute, all right?"

There wasn't time to answer. He didn't bend down exactly; it was more like a swoop, so fast that Abbey, cradled in lazy comfort in the sagging upholstery, couldn't pull herself up and out of the way in time. "Egotistical swine," she muttered, but there wasn't time for more before his lips came to rest on hers.

Humor him, she thought irritably. Very well. What did she have to lose? If the man was so deluded about his skill that he thought kissing her would persuade her to go along with his ridiculous plan, it was time someone straightened him out. Suffering through one more kiss wouldn't hurt her, and once she had made her point . . .

It wasn't one kiss; it was more like hundreds. His mouth was soft and mobile against hers, tasting and sampling for the first few moments as if she were a new food he wasn't quite certain he liked. The moment he made up his mind that he did indeed find her appealing was very obvious; he settled down to a real kiss. Now and then he let the tip of his tongue tease her lips, and more than once his mouth drifted off to another target—temple, earlobe, the soft hollow of her cheek.

During one of those expeditions, Abbey said huskily, "Just what is this all about?"

Flynn didn't answer. He was too busy tracing the arch of her eyebrow.

Abbey shivered a little at the sensation. "If you think this is enough to persuade me to go along with a fake affair..."

He pulled back slightly, his eyes alive with mischief. "I haven't gone quite far enough yet, you mean? Then I'll keep right on." His hand was still propped on the arm of the chair, and his face was barely inches from hers.

He was looking at her lips, which felt swollen and hot. Abbey slid down in the chair and realized too late that the movement could be taken as an invitation. "No!"

Flynn laughed and straightened. "Very well. And I wasn't trying to persuade you, anyway. I just wanted to make sure you didn't think I have *that* much in common with Wayne Marshall." He turned toward the door.

"I'd forgotten all about him," Abbey muttered.

Flynn looked over his shoulder at her, one eyebrow raised quizzically, but he didn't say anything. Instead he pushed open the screen door. "Come in, Sara."

Abbey sat up as suddenly as if one of the old springs in the seat of her chair had given way and jabbed her. She hadn't even heard a knock; was Flynn's hearing simply better than hers, or had she been further out of control than she'd realized?

Sara Merrill came in, blinking in the dimness. "How can you work in light like this, Flynn? You'll blind yourself."

Abbey gratefully remembered the way the subdued lighting had affected her when she'd first arrived; surely even if Sara had been standing at the door for a while she hadn't been able to see anything inside.

"It's not dark over here, so why turn on lights I'm not using?" Flynn led the way across to the easel. "What have you got?"

Sara handed him a big envelope. "The program proofs for Art on the Green. I wanted you to look everything over, especially the lists of artists."

Flynn pulled a couple of closely typed pages out of the envelope and squinted at them. "So if you've spelled a name wrong, I'll have to share the blame?"

"You're too fast for me, Flynn." Sara pulled a chair forward and folded herself up in it. "Hi, Abbey. You're coming to Art on the Green, aren't you?"

Abbey remembered seeing something of the sort in Chandler's calendar of cultural events. "Is it like an open-air gallery?"

"Exactly. We've got artists coming from six states to set up their work on the campus for a day. This will be the biggest show we've had yet."

She sounded proud, Abbey thought. "How long has this been going on, and why haven't I heard of it before?"

"Four years," Sara said.

At the same moment, without even looking up, Flynn added, "It's one of the few annual events in this town in which Janice is not a prime factor, so she probably only mentioned it in passing. The list looks fine, Sara. Did they proof the cover design, too?"

"It's in there." Sara settled back in her chair. "I thought it looked good. The printers said to tell you to come in and talk to them, by the way."

"About this?"

"No, about pulling prints off some of your paintings. They've figured out how to hold the true colors and still keep the price reasonable, if you go with a large-enough quantity."

Flynn shook his head. "Someday, maybe."

"Like when? Now's when you've got the market. Do you know how many prints you could sell just at Art on the Green? Probably a hundred. How many originals do you expect to sell there?"

"Three or four, if I'm lucky."

Sara shrugged. "See?"

"More is not necessarily better, Sara."

"The only easier way to make money would be to print twenty-dollar bills, Flynn. There's nothing criminal about turning a profit."

"Sara, I never expected you to go commercial on me." He slid the proof back into the envelope. "I have this philosophy, you see, that no matter how hard you hug money, it never hugs back—so why worry too much about gathering it in the first place?"

The young professor sniffed. "I happen to know that's not his only eccentricity," she told Abbey. "He cheats at solitaire, too."

"Doesn't everybody?" Flynn said mildly. He returned the envelope to Sara with a dramatic flourish. "Back to you, Madame Chairman. Would you like a soda while we argue about it?"

"I'd love one. Walking across the park is hot work. But I'm not going to argue. If you honestly think that living in a garret makes you more likely to be the next van Gogh, Flynn, there's no point in discussing it at all."

"Good," Flynn said. He raised a questioning eyebrow at Abbey. "A soda?" She nodded, and he went off toward the galley kitchen in the far corner of the room.

"How did you get selected to be in charge of Art on the Green?" Abbey asked. "I'd have expected an art professor."

"Because Sara has good taste and the promotional tactics of a barracuda," Flynn called.

Sara sighed. "The entire art department seems to have managed a summer sabbatical to paint in Italy. Whereas I... Well, Dave Talbot knows what a patsy I am when it comes to Chandler, and he has no hesitation about taking advantage of it. Watch out for that man, Abbey."

"I will. Thanks for the warning."

Sara popped the top on the soda can Flynn handed her and added brightly, "Would you like to help? I'm always looking for warm bodies to hand out programs and things on the day of the festival. And if you've got any spare time in the next couple of weeks..."

Abbey laughed. "Are you sure the only person I should beware of is President Talbot, Sara?"

"I think I resent that."

"Of course I'll help." Abbey reached for the can Flynn offered.

He raised it just beyond her reach. "Is this good enough, or shall I break out the gold-plated goblets?" he asked.

Abbey poked out her tongue at him and grabbed the can. The strong carbonation tickled her throat and made her want to sneeze.

Flynn smothered a grin. "Is that why you always cut your soda with ice? Because you can't take the straight stuff?"

Sara said, "Do you two want to come over for supper and a movie tonight?"

"Sure." Flynn stretched lazily.

Didn't the man ever think? Abbey wondered irritably.
It was natural, she supposed, for Sara to consider them
an item, but for Flynn to feed that impression by answering for Abbey annoyed her no end.

He added, "I'm free, at any rate. What about you,
Abbey?"

Her resentment collapsed like a punctured balloon. She
thought fleetingly about the pile of notes waiting on her
desk and admitted that even if she stayed home she
wasn't likely to work tonight. Anyway, why should she
turn down an invitation that sounded like fun just because Flynn was included? "Yes, I'm free. Mother and
Frank went to visit the old cemeteries this afternoon, so
it's hard to tell when they'll be back."

"That's an original excuse for getting away by themselves," Sara said.

"Some of them are interesting," Flynn argued. "Besides, it's a pretty day for a drive, and there are a lot of
out-of-the-way spots to explore. Five miles down the river
is one of the most gorgeous areas in the Midwest, I think.
We used to camp and fish out there when I was a Boy
Scout."

"You were a Boy Scout?" Abbey hooted. "I suppose
you were in charge of mutinies and revolts in the ranks."

Sara shuddered. "I never could see the fascination in
fishing. Worms and everything. But I suppose if it makes
Frank happy... We're really going to miss him, you
know."

Abbey frowned. "Miss him?"

Sara nodded. "At the apartment complex. He's a
wonder, that man. There's nothing he can't do."

Obviously Sara thought Frank would be moving into
Janice's house. Abbey started to tell her she had nothing
to worry about, but at the last moment she couldn't quite

bring herself to say that her mother was actually giving up her lovely house for a caretaker's apartment. When Janice wanted it known, she would make the announcement.

In any case, there was no opportunity; Sara had gone straight on. "And he's so sweet about it. I dropped my aquamarine ring down the sink a couple of months ago. Frank had to tear the plumbing apart in the whole complex to find it, and he didn't even give me a lecture or tell me how lucky I was to get it back again." She rose and picked up her envelope. "I'd better run. If I'm having a party..."

"Why the hurry?" Flynn said lazily. "It won't take the rest of the afternoon to phone for pizza delivery."

Sara grinned. "You know me very well, don't you? Just for that, you can bring the movie." She rinsed her soda can and left it beside the kitchen sink. "And make sure it's a good one—no ax murders and no sexist garbage. And no spies."

"You could leave me a little latitude," Flynn called after her. "Who knows? You might like ax-murder movies if you actually saw a good one."

Abbey shuddered. "If that's the kind of thing you appreciate, Flynn..."

"All right," Sara said cheerfully. "Bring one, and we'll see who starts to squirm first. I'm betting it'll be you."

Flynn closed the door behind her and came back to his easel. "Sometimes you English-literature types drive me crazy with the attitude that if a lot of people like something, it can't possibly be any good."

"Are we still talking about ax murders?" Abbey said faintly.

"No, she's probably right about that." Flynn anchored a fresh sheet of paper on the work surface. "I couldn't sit still for that kind of blood and gore any more than Sara could. But the idea that something can be good only if the masses think it's incomprehensible is beyond me.''

"I thought Sara's husband writes popular fiction."

"He does. She makes an exception for him. It's the attitude I don't understand. There's nothing wrong with setting out to please a large audience.''

Abbey smiled. "So commercialism is all right in books, but not in art?''

"I wasn't talking about money. I meant enjoyment.''

"More people could enjoy your work if you did prints.''

Flynn looked hurt. "Don't you start on me, Abbey.'' He clipped a small pencil sketch to the upper corner of the easel and reached for a brush.

Abbey drank the rest of her soda in silence while she watched him rough out a ruined castle with an old-fashioned steam engine standing next to it. At least that was what it looked like to her. She started to ask once, but he shushed her, and she remembered his saying that there were times when he didn't like to be interrupted.

Too bad he hadn't let her know he felt that stage coming on, Abbey thought. She would have politely said goodbye and left. As it was, she hated to break his concentration just to tell him she was leaving, so she finished her soda and put her head back against the velvet chair, watching silently as he worked.

By the time she opened her eyes again, only hazily aware that she had dozed off, the steam engine looked even more like a train, but the castle had become a Victorian depot, and the light from the north window beside Flynn's easel was fading fast. She gasped in shock at finding the afternoon gone.

Flynn glanced over his shoulder. "You've been so quiet I almost forgot you were there."

"You told me to shut up."

"Not recently, have I? Are you ready to go?"

Abbey stretched and stood, feeling rather rumpled. "Only if this is a come-as-you-are party."

"Sara's usually are. Very relaxed, no matter how big the crowd."

Abbey tried to smooth the wrinkles out of her linen shorts, but without success. "Is this likely to be big?"

Flynn shrugged. "Hard to tell."

"I'm a little surprised she lives there." Abbey abruptly realized that had not been the most tactful of statements and bit her tongue, but it was too late.

"Why? Feeling a trifle extra-snobbish today?" Flynn's back was to her as he scrubbed paint off his hands at the kitchen sink. The set of his shoulders was inflexible.

Abbey sighed. She searched for the least-troublesome answer and finally settled reluctantly for the truth. "I wasn't making judgments, Flynn. I only meant that since they're both so successful they could live anywhere."

For a while she didn't think he was going to answer. But at last he reached for a towel and said, "Have you considered the possibility that people can be so successful they don't care about appearances?"

"Ouch."

He smiled a little. "I only meant that things don't have to be impressive in order to be nice, or expensive in order to be elegant."

Abbey thought that over while she looked at the watercolor he'd finished earlier. As it dried, the colors had developed the same sort of depth and power that had attracted her to the painting in Ashton Court's dining room.

"You're right about not selling prints," she said.

"What?" Flynn dropped the towel and bent to pick it up. "Why?"

She went on almost to herself. "Unless some printer can figure out a way to capture the luminosity of your work, and the way the light glows on the paper."

Flynn was staring at her.

Abbey felt color rising in her face. What on earth had made her say that? She was no art expert. But it was too late to back out now. "I've never seen anything like it," she said honestly. "I think it's funny that Sara should compare you to van Gogh."

"She was referring to my life-style, not the quality of my work," Flynn said dryly.

"Touchy, aren't you? I *was* talking about your work. You know, I never understood the fascination of van Gogh's paintings. His sunflowers just looked like yellow splotches to me till I saw the original. It practically vibrated on the canvas. And his irises—I swear I could smell them, they were so fresh. But the reproductions, the posters and prints..." She shook her head. "They don't have the same life at all. And neither would yours. It's just not possible to catch that glow and translate it with ordinary ink."

There was a long silence. "Well," Flynn said, "thank you." His voice had an odd catch.

"Anytime," Abbey said. But she didn't quite achieve the flippant tone she'd intended.

The moment of empathy didn't last, of course. By the time they reached the video-rental place, they were already wrangling over which movie to choose.

The critics, Flynn announced, could not be trusted when it came to new releases, so he was holding out for a classic.

Abbey looked at the first one he picked up and wrinkled her nose. "Everyone's seen that a dozen times. If you honestly want a classic, here's a new version of *Hamlet*."

"Sara specified no murders."

"She said no axes. This is a different thing altogether. You can't frown on Shakespeare, Flynn." She looked up at him through her lashes. "Well, maybe you can."

He grinned. "Someday I'll tell you what I really think of Shakespeare." He took the box out of her hand and put it back on the shelf.

Abbey sighed. "Please don't. I can imagine. I don't know why I should have expected any literary appreciation at all from a person who can torture innocent little fish."

"You don't like to fish, either? Very few women do. Maybe it's a genetic defect." He studied the shelves. "Here's a tape on how to improve your trout fishing in six easy lessons. We could take it along just in case you want to broaden your horizons."

Abbey groaned. "I suppose your mother liked that kind of thing?"

She didn't know why she said it. Somewhere along the way, in the years of her childhood, she must have met Flynn's mother, but she had no conscious memory of the woman. And until that moment, she had completely forgotten the fact that Flynn, too, had suffered a loss.

Perhaps, Abbey thought, he felt as strongly about his mother being replaced as she did about her father.

"I'm sorry," she whispered.

Flynn's eyebrows went up, but he didn't ask what she meant.

It was just as well, Abbey thought. She herself didn't know what she was apologizing for. For having no recollection of his mother? Or the fact that she had brought her up at all?

"She didn't mind it," Flynn said thoughtfully. "I think she's still got the family record for biggest fish. And she baited her own hooks, too."

"I can't imagine doing that."

Flynn snorted. "So what did you do on vacations, Abbey? Hang out at Aspen and Disney World?"

"Usually."

"I don't suppose you've ever been camping, have you?"

She decided that riding school wouldn't qualify in his eyes, so she shook her head.

"I wonder..." he said slowly. "I'll bet Janice hasn't, either."

"I doubt it." Something about his tone made her suspicious. "Why?"

"That's the answer. Camping. Get Janice out in the wilds, and show her—"

Abbey's eyes widened. "Show her what Frank will expect! The first time he hands her a hook to bait, she'll faint. You're a genius, Flynn!" She hugged him cheerfully.

"I'm glad you approve."

"Who, me? Of course I..." She paused and then added doubtfully, "You don't need me on this excursion, do you?"

"You would stay at home and send your mother off without a chaperon? Abbey, what kind of girl are you?" He swooped up a handful of videotapes almost at random and took them to the clerk.

"I—Wait a minute, Flynn. If the whole point is to make her feel out of place, then taking me along can't help."

"It's perfect. I will provide the masterful masculine presence, letting Janice know what's expected of her. You can offer tea and sympathy and drive the point home, as you do so well."

Abbey wasn't certain that was a compliment. "I suppose you've already figured out when and where?"

"Oh, out by the river, of course. And as soon as possible. Next weekend, I think. The week after that is Art on the Green, and if we put it off longer we'll be awfully close to the wedding."

Abbey sighed. "All right. With any luck she'll run as soon as she hears about this."

Flynn shook a finger at her. "That is not the proper attitude," he scolded. "This is the second time you haven't shown the least bit of enthusiasm for my plans."

"This one is slightly different from your last brainstorm."

"My point exactly. Still, if you should happen to change your mind about the affair..."

"I won't."

"Just let me know if you'd rather do that than go camping."

Abbey groaned. *What kind of girl are you,* he had asked a few moments ago. Now she knew. When having an affair with Flynn Granger looked like the best alternative she had...

Yes, Abbey told herself. *Crazy* was the only word that fit.

CHAPTER SEVEN

SARA OBVIOUSLY THOUGHT IT the most bizarre idea she had ever heard.

And that's not the half of it, Abbey wanted to say, for Flynn had told Sara just the bare facts, not their reasons for planning the excursion. But the only thing Abbey could do was keep smiling through the discussion. It helped a little, she found, to cross her fingers behind her back in the hope that Janice would set her foot down hard on the whole idea.

But later that night, when Flynn took Abbey home after the movie party, Janice listened to his plan for the weekend and agreed. The only comfort Abbey had was that her mother's enthusiasm was so muted it was almost nonexistent.

Flynn didn't see it quite the same way. "She said it sounded delightful," he reminded Abbey. "Just like an extended picnic."

They were standing on the terrace at the front of the house, and they were supposed to be saying good-night. Abbey shot a look at the dark balcony above. "Watch it," she warned. "Mother's got the hearing of a wild rabbit. Why should you believe what she says, anyway?"

"Why shouldn't I?"

"Because the woman is a champion at smoothing things over, that's why. If she'd been Marie Antoinette, she'd have paused on the guillotine steps and thanked the rabble for inviting her to the party. Believe me, she isn't looking forward to the weekend, no matter what she says."

Flynn grinned. "Well, that's all to the good, wouldn't you say?" He dropped a quick kiss on Abbey's cheek and leapt the two steps from terrace to sidewalk.

"Why did you do that?" she called after him.

Flynn's voice floated back in the soft air. "Think about it, Abbey. You'll find an answer."

She groaned. He had kissed her in case her mother was watching, as well as listening, she concluded, just to shake things up even more.

She was in no better a frame of mind about the whole expedition by Friday, and it didn't help that little things kept going wrong all day. When the computer printer in the Chandler College library jammed late that afternoon and ate a dozen sheets of her expensive rag bond, Abbey muttered a few words she normally didn't admit to knowing.

"Such language," Sara said, coming up to the nearby copy machine with an exam paper to duplicate. "Don't take it out on the printer, please. Our repair budget is all used up."

"I'd like to take it out on Flynn." She reloaded the paper and pushed the feed button. Nothing happened.

"Why? The fishing trip? Honestly, Abbey, can't you find an excuse to stay home?"

Abbey shook her head grimly.

"Well, just roll yourself in poison ivy as soon as you get there, and in three hours you'll be back in town. In the emergency room, of course, getting cortisone shots, but it's better than fishing, right?"

"That's a thought. Thanks."

"Don't thank me. I get enough satisfaction out of simply being helpful." Sara gathered up her exam papers and stood idly tapping them atop the copy machine, watching as Abbey tried the printer again. Then she added more soberly, "Maybe I should keep my mouth shut, but . . ."

Abbey didn't take her eyes off the paper. "But what?"

"I don't think you should take Flynn too seriously, Abbey."

Abbey forgot the printer and stared at Sara in utter astonishment. "Take him seriously? What on earth do you mean?"

Sara turned slightly pink, but the expression in her eyes was one of gentle determination. "I don't think you should count on this being any more than just a summer romance. Flynn's a wonderful guy, but I'm afraid he's not the settling-down sort."

Abbey's jaw dropped so hard that she had to remind herself to close her mouth. "I'm perfectly aware of that," she managed to say. "But—"

"It would be pretty awful if you were to get hurt," Sara persisted. "Having to face him at every family gathering wouldn't be easy."

"Don't fret. I'm perfectly safe." Abbey's voice was just a bit crisper than she'd intended.

Sara nodded. "Forgive me for butting in. I know it's none of my business, but I'm worried about you."

It was all Abbey could do to keep from telling her about Flynn's original plan. Hearing of his rationale for an affair would at least put to rest Sara's fears about Abbey's being taken in. And it would serve Flynn right if Sara was incensed enough to give him a lecture. . . .

No. It would be like opening Pandora's box, Abbey told herself. So she settled for soothing reassurance and started for home, leaving Sara still looking doubtful.

The books and papers she was carrying were heavy, and she paused on a street corner to shift her load just as a car stopped beside her. "Need a lift?" Boyd asked.

Abbey gratefully climbed in. "Thanks. It's a bit warm for hauling these around." She gestured to the stack balanced in her lap. "What are you doing out of the office at this hour, anyway? Playing hooky?"

"Dropping papers off to a very important client."

Of course, Abbey thought. It wasn't a free afternoon or surely he'd have shed the oh-so-correct tie and maybe even his jacket.

"If I'm lucky, I'll be out of the office on schedule tonight. How about dinner?"

"I can't." The regret in Abbey's voice was real. The cool, charming dining room at the country club sounded very inviting. As it was, she'd probably be eating hot dogs charred over an open fire.

"Tomorrow?"

Abbey shook her head.

"It wouldn't have to be dinner. We could play tennis or something in the afternoon."

"I'm tied up all weekend."

"I see," Boyd said slowly. "Flynn Granger again, no doubt."

"Boyd, you know perfectly well that I'm not dating Flynn."

"I know you're certainly spending lots of time with him. Whenever I call, it seems, you're not available because of Flynn."

That was true, Abbey reflected. When Boyd had called on Sunday evening, she had been at the Merrills' with

Flynn. On Tuesday he had left a message with her mother because Abbey had been at Flynn's garage plotting strategy and watching him finish the painting of the depot and train. And last night, she'd been at home, but Flynn had been eating cookies in the kitchen, and he had answered the telephone when Boyd called.

Dammit, Abbey thought. It was bad enough that half the town was going around with the wrong idea about her and Flynn, but it was especially unjust when it came to Boyd. How was she to discover if the man was important to her when she was always too busy with Flynn's little schemes even to talk to him?

But before she could decide just how much of an explanation was possible, Boyd shrugged. "It's your right. If Flynn Granger is the kind of companion you find fascinating . . ."

Abbey's desire to make things clear to Boyd evaporated. She could certainly understand why he was confused, but if he were going to drown himself in self-pity, he could just go jump in the river!

The thought of the river reminded her of the camping trip once more. The very idea gave her heartburn, and she was scowling when she got out of the car.

"I'll see you some other time," she said. "Thanks for the ride."

In the kitchen, Norma was bustling about putting things in the wicker picnic hamper that stood open on the kitchen table. "Don't forget your sunscreen," she was telling Janice. "And insect repellent. And the antibiotic cream . . ."

"This is not an expedition to the outback, Norma." Janice turned to Abbey. "I'm glad you're home, dear. Flynn said he'd be over to get you in a few minutes. In fact, I thought I heard a car door."

"Boyd brought me home."

"He's a very nice young man, isn't he?" Janice said absently. "Have you finished packing?"

"What's to pack?"

"That's good."

Abbey eyed her in disbelief. *She didn't even hear what I said,* she realized.

"I'm looking forward to this," Janice said.

Abbey thought she sounded more determined than enthusiastic. And that was all to the good. If Janice was already having to force herself to keep her spirits up...

With any luck, we might be home by midnight!

Janice took a package of steaks out of the refrigerator and put it in an insulated cooler.

Abbey eyed the banged-up corners and scratched paint of the metal cooler. It looked as if it had been around the world at least twice, and not first-class. "Where did you get that thing, Mom?"

"It's Frank's. I swear I had a bottle of steak sauce in my hand," Janice muttered. "Now where have I..."

"Sounds like we're taking all the comforts of home," Abbey said, picking the bottle up from its hiding place behind the wicker picnic basket. "In fact, it looks like we're taking the whole kitchen. I've got a better idea. Why don't we just stop at the country club for dinner first?"

Flynn said from behind her, "Bite your tongue, Abbey."

She felt herself coloring a little. He was right; the whole point would be lost if the weekend were comfortable and free of annoyance. Still, he'd better be careful what he said, too, or Janice was bound to get suspicious.

"A steak never tastes as good anywhere as it does outdoors," Flynn went on. "Grilled over an open fire..."

"And seasoned with mosquitoes," Abbey said under her breath.

He grinned, but didn't argue. Instead, he kissed Janice's cheek and said, "Actually, all we really need to survive is salt and pepper. We'll teach you to fish for the rest."

Abbey shuddered.

Flynn added gently, "I've seen the day when we've had that cooler filled to the brim with fresh-caught fish."

Abbey frowned. "I devoutly hope it's been washed since then."

Flynn's eyes acquired a wicked sparkle. "We just catch them and gut them and throw them in on ice."

Abbey turned toward the nearest cabinet. "I hope you remembered the peanut butter, Mom. And lots of cheese and crackers."

"If you're going to be stubborn, we'll stop on the way out of town and pick up some tofu," Flynn said. "But you might want to change clothes first. You aren't going to be very comfortable on my motorcycle in that skirt."

Abbey closed her eyes in pain. "Why the motorcycle?"

"Because there isn't room for all of us in Dad's truck. Besides, we've been assigned to get the fire started, so if you want your dinner at a reasonable hour, you'd better hurry."

She didn't hurry, and by the time she came down the back stairs in jeans, carrying a duffel bag, the chaos in the kitchen had been reduced to mere confusion. Flynn put her bag on the pile waiting to be loaded, seized another handful of cookies and started for the door.

Abbey looked warily at the motorcycle. She hadn't paid much attention to it before; since bikes were not her chosen mode of transportation, they had never held any interest for her. Now that a ride seemed unavoidable, she couldn't help thinking that this particular motorcycle had grown since the last time she'd seen it.

Flynn poked a cookie in Abbey's mouth and handed her a helmet.

"Is this thing safe?" she asked indistinctly.

"Does that mean you've never been on one before? You deprived child."

"Why can't we just take a car?"

"Because we need the truck to haul stuff."

Abbey nodded. There was not only the picnic basket and the cooler, but she'd seen at least two boxes full of staples and supplies. Janice might have been packing for a month in the wilderness. "Well, at least we won't starve," Abbey said philosophically.

"Which you might if you had to depend on fishing for your dinner." Flynn strapped his helmet on and climbed onto the bike. "Come."

Abbey stayed stubbornly on the sidewalk. "I understand why Frank needs the truck. But we could take my car, couldn't we?"

"You don't want your car to go some of the places we're headed."

What a comforting notion that was, Abbey thought. She surrendered and put on the helmet, and as the motorcycle roared down the driveway she shouted, "Besides, this way we can talk, right?"

Flynn grinned at her over his shoulder. "Something like that," he called back. "Hang on!"

He took the highway out of town, and after a few miles of smooth paved roads, Abbey began to relax. Riding a motorcycle was probably never going to be her favorite pastime, but it wasn't as bad as she'd expected. The helmet wasn't annoyingly hot or heavy, and she found that the battering pressure of the wind whipping her clothes could be reduced by keeping her body pressed close to Flynn's.

Her arms tightened a little around his waist. The solid feel of him was comforting, and it was warmer that way, too. She closed her eyes and let her body nestle naturally against his back. The fuzzy surface of his flannel shirt tickled her cheek, and his ribs were hard under her hands.

Ten miles from town, they left the highway and began to wind down a narrow country road. Chalky dust from the rock surface rolled out beneath the bike's wheels and formed a plume behind them. If they stopped, Abbey thought, she'd probably choke to death before the dust settled.

But soon they left the gravel and turned down a grassy lane. Abbey had just opened her mouth to ask how far they were going when the motorcycle hit the first bump, and she bit her tongue hard. By the time she could talk again, Flynn had pulled the cycle to a stop under the biggest oak tree Abbey had ever seen.

"I'm glad you didn't take that last stretch any faster," she said thickly.

"And take a chance on wrecking my toy? Those bumps are why we didn't drive your car. Besides, all that gravel is terrible on the paint."

"I'm not worried about paint at the moment. I think my teeth are loose." She ran the tip of her tongue experimentally across them.

Flynn watched her silently. Abbey was almost disappointed that he didn't have a snappy comment. She pulled off her helmet and looked around.

To the right, beyond a long slope full of trees, she could see the gleam of the river. The only sound was the muted murmur of the current, and the only building to be seen was a small metal shed not far from the giant oak tree. Nearby was a weathered picnic table and a brick fire pit. There were no cabins, no playground, no electrical hookups.

"This is a public park?" she said.

Flynn frowned. "Where did you get that idea? Dad owns this land. Didn't I tell you that?"

"No, you didn't."

"He's had it for years. That's why the Boy Scouts could spend so much time here."

Abbey released a long sigh. "I gathered you didn't go in for air-conditioned recreational vehicles. But..."

Flynn made a face. "I never have understood why people pack their television sets and stereos and gas grills and then go park in a concrete campground three feet from the next camper and say they're getting away from it all. As far as I'm concerned—"

Abbey interrupted ruthlessly. "But I expected a cabin, at least. Is it asking too much to want a roof in case it rains?"

"Dad's bringing the tents." He started toward the metal shed. "Besides, it's not going to rain. Look at that sky."

Abbey looked. The peaceful white clouds floating above didn't hold any particular messages for her. She went after Flynn, her running shoes sliding in the rocky soil. "Tents? I suppose that means we sleep on the ground?"

"Don't panic. He's got air mattresses and sleeping bags. Grab some wood, will you?"

"Air mattresses. What a comfort."

Flynn shrugged. "You had a choice, remember? You could have gone along with my first plan."

"It would never have worked."

"How do you know? You wouldn't give it a fair chance."

"It would have been useless. I'd have murdered you before the first week was out."

"And you think that wouldn't have broken up our parents' romance?" He handed her a split chunk of wood. "I can see it now—your mother weeping softly at your trial, while my father tells the jury how a vicious female robbed him of a loving son—"

Abbey snapped her fingers. "That's the answer! I knew there was a great idea I was missing." She shifted the wood till she was holding it like a club. "No, this is too big to get a good grip." She put it aside and poked through the pile for a longer, thinner weapon.

Flynn's eyebrows raised. "You sound awfully experienced. Are you in the habit of displaying homicidal tendencies?"

"Only when you're around." She gave up her search and gathered an armload of logs.

"Still," Flynn said almost to himself, "maybe I should talk to the person who shares your apartment in Minneapolis."

"Shared," Abbey corrected.

"Oh? You had a fight, I presume?"

"No. I'm just not planning on my next job being in the Twin Cities, that's all." She dumped her load of wood next to the pit.

"Ah. Lover's quarrel."

"Not at all. It wasn't even a roommates' spat. Why would you assume I was sharing my apartment with a man, anyway?"

"You weren't?"

"No. Not that it's any business of yours. Keep it up and I'll go back to looking for a weapon."

"Try this one," Flynn recommended, handing her a branch three inches in diameter. "It's oak, and guaranteed to be harder than my head."

"Thank you. I'll keep it in reserve." Abbey put the branch carefully off to one side and carried another armful of wood over to the fire pit. She sat down on the brick edge and watched as Flynn assembled a pile of wood shavings and twigs and set it ablaze.

"You use matches?" she asked, feigning horror. "I thought you were the sort of purist who would insist on rubbing two sticks together, but it seems you've surrendered to modern conveniences. I'm terribly disappointed."

The look he shot her could have set paper smoldering. Abbey laughed and went after more wood. At this rate, she thought, camping might turn out to be fun, after all.

SHE SUSPECTED, when Frank began taking lawn chairs from the truck, that he had made definite concessions to the presence of ladies in his camp, and the look on Flynn's face as he watched his father unload a big beach umbrella confirmed it.

"He's getting soft in his old age," Flynn muttered.

"Perhaps he realized that Mother was never a Boy Scout."

Flynn eyed Abbey warily. "Shouldn't you be worried?"

"Why? It would take a lot more than a chair and a spot of shade to make this a comfortable experience." She went off to help Janice unpack the picnic basket.

"You forgot your swimsuit, Abbey," her mother said. "It's a good thing I checked your room again and saw it."

"I didn't forget. I just didn't think I'd need it."

"Does that mean you'd rather skinny-dip?" Flynn asked.

Abbey glared at him. "I wasn't intending to swim in the river at all."

"Why not?" Flynn asked. "There's an inlet right at the foot of the hill where the water is amazingly calm. It's perfectly safe—as long as you've got a buddy, that is. I'll be happy to be yours."

Abbey didn't answer that. She thought Janice looked startled enough as it was, and there was no sense in giving Flynn a chance to enlarge on the topic.

The evening was pleasantly warm, and the breeze whispered softly through the branches of the huge old oak. Still, Abbey felt dusty and sticky from the ride, and the thought of cool water rushing over her was an inviting one. It was tempting when, shortly after dinner, Flynn stretched and said he believed he'd go for a swim. But she stayed stubbornly in her chair a few feet from where Frank and Janice were playing cribbage. She suspected Flynn considered swimsuits in the same category as televisions, stereos and gas grills—fine in their place, but inappropriate for camping.

He hadn't returned yet when Janice began to yawn steadily. "All this fresh air makes me sleepy," she said, and tossed down her cards.

Frank grinned. "Are you sure you're sleepy? Or just tired of losing?"

Janice gave him a playful swat and then bent to kiss him.

The caress was a long one, and Abbey ducked her head to keep from watching. "I think I'll turn in, too," she announced, and followed her mother to the tent the men had put up for them. As an afterthought, she asked Frank, "All that food won't attract wild animals, will it?"

"Oh, I expect the raccoons will be curious. But don't fret. They're nosy but harmless unless they're threatened."

"Don't worry about me threatening them," Abbey murmured, and Frank grinned.

She zipped the tent flap and crouched for a moment in the limited space looking doubtfully at the narrow air mattress. She sighed and tugged off her jeans and shirt, then crawled into her sleeping bag. It had a faint aroma, not unpleasant at all but hard to define, but before she had managed to analyze it, she was fast asleep.

Morning found her snuggled deep in the bag; overnight the temperature had dropped, and the tip of her nose felt cold. She stretched experimentally and found a few muscles she hadn't known she possessed. Altogether, however, she didn't feel bad.

On the other side of the tent, Janice was groaning. "I think I'm getting rheumatism," she said. "Even my elbows ache."

"It's not exactly the Ritz, you're right." Abbey sat up and wriggled out of the bag, shivering a little. "But at least no snakes came to visit last night. I'll bet there are plenty around."

Janice stretched. "No doubt. Still, it's great out here, isn't it? Listen to the birds. Frank's trying to teach me to identify their calls. Without much success yet, I'm afraid."

Despite herself, Abbey had to admire her mother's spunk. "You're taking this well," she said. She rummaged in her duffel bag for a fresh shirt and reached for her jeans.

Janice stopped brushing her hair. "Why shouldn't I? We're going to live out here, you know."

The comment caught Abbey in the most awkward position possible, and her foot jammed in the narrow-cut jeans. She was already off balance in the low tent; the surprise sent her sprawling onto the air mattress. "What? Here?" She looked wildly around the little tent. "Mother, you can't!"

"Oh, not like this of course," Janice said hastily. "Camping trips are one thing, but I couldn't handle a tent for long and Frank knows it. We're going to build a log cabin."

"A cabin?" Abbey's voice was little more than an echo.

"Yes. We've staked out the site already."

Abbey straightened her tangle of clothes. Her hands were shaking, and it took concentration to finish getting dressed.

"Don't look so horrified, Abbey. Log cabins come in kits these days, with laundry rooms and sun porches."

"But Mother..." Abbey bit her lip and started over. "I don't understand." She felt as if she were talking to a very small, very unreasonable child.

Janice was powdering her nose. "It seemed a sensible compromise. Frank loves to be outdoors and I insist on a real house. So the cabin struck us as the perfect—"

"But to live all the way out here! It's silly. You'll be on the road all the time, Mother. Whenever you have a committee meeting it will take half the day to get to town and back."

"No," Janice said. "I'm going to give all that up."

Abbey supposed it were a good thing she was already sitting down. It saved the air mattress another blow. "All of it?"

Janice nodded. "I've already resigned from the garden club. Once the summer flower show is over, I'm finished. The other committees and clubs are mostly inactive till fall, so there'll be time to find people to take over. Boyd's going to fill my spot as secretary of the alumni committee, and—"

"Why?"

Janice's eyebrows went up. "Boyd's a perfectly capable young man. Oh, you mean why I'm quitting everything." She brushed on a touch of lipstick and closed the compact with a snap.

"You've always enjoyed those things. Why would you give them up now? It's Frank who's making you do this, isn't it?"

"It doesn't have much to do with Frank, you know." Janice's voice was firm. "Oh, incidentally it does of course. If it wasn't for Frank, I'd probably have run the flower show till I was ninety. But—"

"That's what I mean." Abbey took a deep breath and put a hand on her mother's arm. "If Frank is so jealous of you that he wants you to give up all your other interests—"

"He doesn't. I don't think you understand, Abbey. I only did those things because I needed something to fill my time. Your father was always so busy, and it was a way I could occupy myself and help his career at the same time by being visible in the community. Then after he died and you were away at school, there was even more of a hole that needed filling. But I'm tired of all that. It's time for someone else to take over."

"So you can look after Frank?"

"No," Janice said gently. "So Frank and I can enjoy the time we have together."

Abbey groaned. "I know you think that's going to be enough, but—"

"I won't be bored, you know," Janice went on cheerfully. "The cabin is a kit, so we're going to do a great deal of the work ourselves. We should have it ready by winter."

Abbey put her head in her hands.

Janice moved around the tent for a couple of minutes, and then came to sit quietly beside her. "Please try to understand that I am not doing this just to annoy you."

"Mother, I cannot approve."

Janice sighed. "I'm not asking for your approval, Abbey. I don't need it. I would like you to be happy for me, but even if you can't, you still must accept that I have a right to make my own choices."

Her tone of voice was one Abbey remembered well from the disciplinary chats of her childhood, but it had been years since Janice had used it. Abbey felt tears welling up.

We used to be close, she wanted to shout. *Before all this happened. Before Frank got in the way. Before you changed. . . .*

But there was no way to change things back. It was obvious to Abbey that Janice was making a grave error. But it was equally obvious that any further attempt to stop her was only going to increase the tension between them. Ultimately the damage would be too severe to patch up. And if that happened, Abbey would have lost not only her father, but her mother, as well.

And the second loss would be largely her own fault.

Tears weighed her lashes down till she couldn't even blink them away. She brushed her shirtsleeve carelessly across her eyes. "All right," she said in little more than a whisper. "You win." She stumbled to her feet.

"Abbey—"

"I'm going for a walk." She flung the words over her shoulder and burst out of the tent.

Frank looked up from the cast-iron skillet he was just putting over the fire, and Abbey saw a frown of concern gather between his brows. Flynn, standing nearby, looked stunned. Abbey lowered her head and charged off into the trees.

Flynn started after her, but Janice caught his arm. "No," she said. "Let her go. She needs a little time, that's all."

A little time, Abbey thought. As if that were going to solve anything.

But at least there was one advantage. She didn't have to face Flynn just yet, and explain to him that she was deserting the cause.

CHAPTER EIGHT

THE UNDERGROWTH had been cut back in spots, forming a rough trail, and Abbey followed it blindly. From the bottom of the ridge, it hadn't seemed much of a climb at all, but by the time she reached the top, she was out of breath and her chest was aching.

There was a large fallen tree right at the edge of a clearing that overlooked the valley. Abbey climbed up onto it and settled herself in the fork between the trunk and a huge branch. From her perch, she could catch just a glimpse of the river, shining silver in the sunlight, its current relentless and unalterable.

Very much like this entire situation, she thought.

She put her head back against the dry, scaly bark and listened to the gradual slowing of her heartbeat. Eventually the quiet of the day seeped into her. It didn't bring her peace of mind; nothing, she thought, was likely to do that. But at least there was a measure of relief in not fighting the impossible anymore.

She sat there for a long time, watching the quiet clouds drift by, thinking sadly of her father and how different things would have been if Warren had lived.

"It's not my responsibility," Abbey told herself. "I can't stop Mother from doing what she pleases."

She repeated it so often that finally it took on some of the soothing qualities of a mantra. And at last, under its influence, she relaxed a little. She might even have dozed off, for she certainly didn't hear the second walker in the woods until he stood directly under her perch.

"Hi," Flynn said.

Abbey had to grab for a branch to keep her balance. "What are you doing here?"

"When you didn't come back for lunch, Janice got worried."

"How did you find me?"

"It wasn't difficult. You left a trail even an amateur couldn't lose." He looked up at her for a long moment, his eyes narrowed against the strong sunlight. "Do you want to come down and talk about it?"

The question was gentle, but it set Abbey's nerves on edge nevertheless. "Not really."

He backed off a few feet and studied the fallen tree, then grabbed a branch and easily pulled himself up beside her. "I don't want to get a stiff neck while we talk," he explained as he settled down on the wide trunk.

Abbey didn't look at him. She was bracing herself for a grilling. When he learned she had surrendered...

Flynn leaned against a branch and looked out across the valley. "It's peaceful up here, isn't it, with the breeze and the water sparkling in the sunshine." His voice was lazy, soothing, almost hypnotic. "The aroma drifting through is wild roses. Did you see the whole hillside of them over there? And look..."

Abbey followed the direction of his pointing finger. Down the hill just a little, a rabbit had emerged from a clump of grass and stopped to sniff warily. Its nose twitched for a while, then, apparently deciding the scent of humans was too faint to be a threat, it began to feed on a patch of clover.

"Its nose is so flexible it's almost like rubber," Abbey said. "I never dreamed—"

"Shush." Flynn sat up slowly.

For half a minute Abbey couldn't even see what he was watching. Then from the shadow of a tree, a doe moved silently into the clearing and paused to look around.

Abbey was still holding her breath when she saw a smaller, less cautious shadow appear from the shadows in response to some silent signal from the doe. The fawn was less graceful than its mother, not quite certain of its still-spindly legs. It wasn't very old; the camouflage spots were still distinctly visible.

"I thought deer only came out after dusk." Abbey's voice was little more than a whisper.

Flynn shook his head a fraction.

The doe moved off along the edge of the clearing and vanished into the trees again. The fawn trailed at a safe distance, waiting to be summoned, but obviously distracted now and then by the wonders of his new world.

When they were gone, Abbey sighed. "Their eyes are like liquid velvet."

"Once, at midnight, I saw a whole herd of them up here," Flynn said. "They were playing tag, just like kids."

"I had no idea how beautiful they are close up. Thanks, Flynn. I'd probably have scared them away before I ever saw them."

Flynn turned slowly toward her.

Abbey read his intention in his eyes and uttered a murmur of protest. But he didn't seem to hear, and there was little else Abbey could do to stop him. She told herself it would be undignified to leap out of the tree. Besides, she had survived his kisses before, hadn't she? And certainly she was safe from anything more at the moment, as long as they were precariously perched five feet off the ground. So she closed her eyes and submitted.

The problem, she realized within half a minute, was that it wasn't really accurate to call it a kiss. Slow-motion seduction was more like it. As Flynn's mouth moved gently against hers, Abbey's body roused to delicious thrills of sensation in much the same way that a limb, long deprived of blood, prickles back to life as circulation is restored. And when his hands slipped gently under her T-shirt to stroke her skin, the prickles inside her grew to a sensuous agony that left her shivering with longing.

"Too bad we don't even have an air mattress at the moment," Flynn murmured against her lips. "There's a nice batch of moss, though...."

Sanity seeped back into Abbey's brain. "It wouldn't matter if you had a four-poster handy," she managed to whisper. "I'm not the sort for casual romps."

Flynn raised his head and gave her a skeptical look, but the dangerous moment had passed and Abbey's conscience had reasserted itself. And just in the nick of time, she admitted. There was something about this man that was addictive.

She extracted herself from his embrace with difficulty; it wasn't that he tried to hold her against her will, but Abbey was feeling slightly dizzy, and it would have been easier to continue to lean against him. "Remember?" she said, trying to keep her tone playful. "I said no to the whole idea of an affair. Besides, since we're going to be relatives of a sort...."

"Don't you think that just adds some illicit spice to the idea?" But he sounded as if he were arguing from habit rather than conviction.

Abbey took a deep breath. "I mean it, you know. We *are* going to be relatives. I just gave Mother my blessing, Flynn."

"You what?"

She lost her nerve. "Well, sort of, at least. I didn't exactly have any choice left, don't you see? I don't mean I approve, because I don't and I never will, but I told her I wouldn't fight it anymore. So unless some miracle happens..."

"How gracious of you."

There was a note in his voice she didn't quite recognize, and it puzzled her.

"Giving them permission, like the grand lady of the manor granting a favor to the peasants. Well, give yourself a medal, Abbey, but don't expect one from me."

"Flynn! Just because I've accepted the inevitable..."

He shook his head. "You haven't accepted anything at all. Don't you even see the difference? You've condescended to give them permission—as if you had the power to direct their lives. And now I suppose you're going to sit in a corner and sulk and remind them for the next umpteen years of how unhappy they've made you. Can't you even get out of their way, Abbey? Stop trying to make them feel guilty, and give them a fair chance!"

The blood was pounding in her ears at the rank injustice of that accusation, and at something else, as well—the abrupt realization that all along he had been manipulating her, influencing her plans, spying and intriguing against her.

"So the truth finally comes out," she said bitterly. "You're in favor of this marriage, after all. This whole weekend was aimed at me, wasn't it? You must have known Frank and Mother have been coming out here all along. Did you all get together to plan it, I wonder?"

"I haven't said a word to either of them." Flynn sighed and ran his fingers through his hair. "Abbey, I told you at the beginning precisely where I stood. They're adults, and I have no opinion on what they should do."

"Oh, really? And is that why you've been sabotaging me all along—because you were so solidly neutral? Dammit, Flynn, don't lie to me!"

"All right, I won't. At first, I almost agreed with you. They're a weird combination, and I admit it. But you were treating them like children who needed discipline, and after a while, I began to feel sympathetic to their cause. They seem perfectly happy—at least when you're not around. Who's to say it can't work? Besides, I generally side with the underdog."

"Of course you would," Abbey said nastily. "Because you'll always be one!"

The words were no sooner out than she regretted them. It was a cruel thing to say, no matter what the provocation. Even if she had believed the words, it would have been unforgivable to utter them.

But in fact, she was far from believing what she'd said. Flynn had an incredible talent, that was true. It was not his art, however, but his fierce independence of mind that would keep him a winner. Even if he were to live in a tarpaper shack on the thin edge of hunger, Flynn Granger would never be deprived or disadvantaged—because he would simply refuse to see himself that way.

He looked at her for one long moment, while the razor-sharp words still hung in the air between them, and then he leapt down from the tree and plunged across the clearing.

Abbey called, "Flynn!"

He must have heard. But he was gone.

She put her face down against the rough bark of the tree trunk and closed her eyes. It didn't help much, for the world still seemed to be swinging in erratic circles. She almost welcomed the harsh scrape of bark against her cheek. At least it helped take her mind off the sick emptiness in the pit of her stomach.

No matter what the provocation, it had been a rotten thing to say. No, she told herself, it was even worse than that. It had been stupid, too. The only thing she'd managed to do was confirm to Flynn that she really was the heartless, snobbish, insensitive twit he had said she was.

"But I'm not like that," she whispered. "Not really." Hot angry tears sprang to her eyes. Flynn hadn't even tried to understand how she felt about all this. . . .

The tears burned themselves away eventually, but the nausea remained, born of a harsh truth she could no longer refuse to face—the knowledge that Flynn had understood her all too well. He was absolutely right; she *was* selfish and childish and not very nice.

Her soul ached at the idea of coming face-to-face with this side of herself. But what hurt even more, somehow, was the idea that she hadn't been able to see it for herself. Someone else had looked into the dark corners of her heart and pointed out her flaws, and she didn't like it.

She especially didn't like the idea that it had been Flynn. She could have taken it from her mother; that sort of thing was a parent's job. But for Flynn to turn on her like this . . . Abbey almost felt betrayed.

"I thought he liked me," she whispered. "We were pals. And now this."

But there was no changing what had happened. She sat up straight and dried her eyes, brushing the loose bits of bark off her face as best she could.

"It doesn't matter what he thinks of me," Abbey told herself firmly.

But there was a tiny curl of fear in the bottom of her stomach, and a suspicion that it mattered a lot more than she was willing to admit.

WHEN SHE CAME BACK into camp at midafternoon, neither Frank nor Flynn was anywhere to be seen. Janice lowered her paperback, gave Abbey one quick comprehensive look and said, "You're here just in time to help me with dinner."

Abbey, who had expected a barrage of questions, was grateful to get a matter-of-fact assignment instead. She picked up a knife and quietly began cutting up a head of cauliflower. "Did Frank and Flynn go fishing or something?"

"Frank did." Janice opened a bag of carrots. "Flynn went back to town."

Abbey blinked in surprise.

"Didn't he tell you about his appointment? He'd forgotten that he was to see a client tonight about a commission."

"I wouldn't want him to miss that," Abbey managed to say.

So he had returned to camp with an easy story, she thought, and he hadn't even told Janice that they had quarreled. Abbey didn't know whether to be pleased, or even surprised. She hadn't been looking forward to facing him, that was for sure. And yet...

Without him, all the sparkle had vanished from the camping trip. There would be no more banter over how to build a fire, no more teasing over whether she was going to bait a hook, no more quiet moments of watching animals....

I don't want him to be gone, Abbey admitted. *And I don't want him to be angry with me. I want things back the way they were.* But she hadn't the vaguest idea how to go about it.

After dinner Janice sat down by the fire and picked up her book. Frank stretched out in the lounge chair next to her with a piece of wood and a pocketknife. Abbey, who had nothing to occupy either her hands or her thoughts, found herself watching as the chunk of dark-grained wood began to take shape under the sharp blade of the knife.

"How do you decide what it's going to be?" she asked finally.

Frank looked up as if he wasn't quite certain she was talking to him. "Each piece of wood has a special feel to it," he said. "It tells me what it wants to be. I just tinker with it until it seems right."

His hands showed no sign of hesitation as he pared off slivers of wood here and there. The shape grew more defined as Abbey watched, and within half an hour it became a brooding human figure, head bent in despair.

Flynn had said she was trying to make them feel guilty. He hadn't been entirely correct about that, for Abbey hadn't set out to make anyone miserable—not consciously, at least. Still, it was obvious that Frank wasn't happy about the situation as it stood, and that distress was pouring out of him through his knife.

"That's what you call tinkering?" Abbey said. "It's beautiful."

Frank set the knife aside and held the figure up to study it. "It's not anything special," he said, and raised his hand as if to toss the bit of wood into the fire.

Abbey said sharply. "Don't! May I have it?"

Frank shrugged and gave it to her.

It was still warm from his fingers. In the fading light she studied the rough little figure and wondered how a single line etched into the face could convey such an expression of pain.

"Mother's jewelry box," she said suddenly. "You carved it, too, didn't you?"

Frank nodded.

"It's very different. Ornate and smoother and more finished. But this reminds me of the way you carved the rosebud with just a few strokes. It looks so perfect and complete, as if it even has the aroma."

After a little silence, Frank said gruffly, "I made one for you, too. Your mother thought... Well, it doesn't matter."

She thought I wasn't ready to appreciate it, Abbey reflected. And she was right.

She closed her fingers tightly around the little figure in her hand. She could make both Frank and Janice very happy right now, she thought, simply by asking for the box that was already hers. And when Flynn heard about it, he would see that she really was trying, that she wasn't keeping herself aloof....

But something held her back. It wouldn't be quite honest somehow, she thought, if she accepted Frank's gift when she had not yet completely accepted him. And Flynn, if he bothered to comment at all, wouldn't hesitate to tell her she was being a hypocrite.

She heard herself say, "I'll let you know when I'm ready for it."

Frank smiled a little, as if he had read her mind. "You do that, Abbey."

There seemed nothing else to say. Abbey jumped up and went over to her mother's chair. "You're going to ruin your eyes reading in this light, Janice Stafford," she said. "Want to go for a walk with me?"

For an instant, Janice looked wary, and Abbey's heart sank. Then Janice put her book aside. "Of course. Where shall we go?"

Abbey released a quiet sigh of relief. "How about showing me where you're going to build the cabin?"

They strolled along in the twilight in almost complete silence. Janice seemed disinclined to speak at all, and Abbey was afraid to start talking. Was it already too late to find their way back to their old closeness?

Janice stopped in the center of a clearing. "Here," she said. "It's far enough from the river to be safe no matter how high the water gets, but close enough to have the view. And we won't need to cut down many trees."

"It's beautiful, Mom."

Janice didn't seem to hear. "The front of the house will face the river, so we can take advantage of passive solar heating in the winter, and it will use all the energy-efficient—"

Abbey reached out to touch her mother's arm. "I really mean that. I'm not just saying it."

Even in the dim light she could see the mist gathering in Janice's eyes. "I appreciate your change of heart, honey."

Abbey said hastily, "It's not like magic. But I'm trying."

"That's all I ask." Janice bit her lip and whispered, "I need you, Abbey...."

Something deep inside Abbey seemed to crack. "Do you know you've never said that before?"

"That I need you? But of course I do, darling!" She pulled Abbey into her arms. "Whatever gave you the idea I didn't?"

Abbey shook her head against her mother's shoulder. "I don't know. You never seemed to need anyone. Even when Daddy died, you just went straight on."

"You thought I didn't miss him?"

"Not exactly." Abbey was groping for a way to express something she had never tried to put into words before. "But I thought you didn't want me around. You sent me back to school."

"Oh, Abbey, no!" Janice sank down on a log. "I was accustomed to being alone. I was afraid if I let you stay, I'd grow dependent on you, and I'd smother you and want to hang on to you forever—all the things mothers aren't supposed to do."

Abbey was frowning. "What do you mean, you were accustomed to being alone? You had Daddy!"

"Yes, my dear, I had Warren, who never worked less than a twelve-hour day in all the years we were married. Is it any wonder I took up every cause that came along? I had to do something with all my time." She looked down at her hands, fingers locked together. "I'm sorry, darling. I've tried never to talk about it, because I didn't want to be a complainer, or sound as if I was trying to belittle your father. Every marriage has its compromises, and even though I sometimes felt I made more than my share, I was never unhappy about my choice. Warren was a very special man. But I can't let you hold him up as a saint."

"Because it isn't fair to Frank to compare him to Daddy?"

Janice shook her head. "No. It's far more important than that, Abbey. It isn't fair to the man you'll someday marry, if you carry an unrealistic image of your father."

Like most soon-to-be brides, Janice seemed to have marriage on the brain. "You don't need to worry about that,'' Abbey muttered. ''My wedding day is a long time off.''

FLYNN STILL HADN'T come back to the river by the time they broke camp on Sunday afternoon, and Abbey was getting worried. He should have been over his irritation by now, she thought. He'd said his piece and got it off his chest. And as for what she had said, well, she could hardly tell him she was sorry when he was nowhere to be seen. Sooner or later he had to give her a chance to apologize, didn't he?

It would be all right, she told herself. It wasn't like Flynn to hold a grudge. He must have realized by now how angry she'd been, and that she hadn't really meant it, and as soon as she had a chance to tell him so, they could get things back to normal.

She just hoped it was soon, because the longer she thought about their quarrel, the worse the bruises on her self-esteem became. By the time she'd showered off the weekend's accumulated grime, rehearsing her speech all the while, she'd decided there was no time like the present.

She came downstairs in fresh shorts and shirt, still combing her wet hair. ''I'm going for a walk, Mom,'' she said, and then saw with dismay that Janice was restoring the kitchen to order. Good manners said she should help rather than leave the mess for Norma tomorrow, but she had her heart set on finding Flynn.

She sighed and pitched in to help. Flynn would have to wait.

It was surprising how fast the work went. ''Thanks, dear,'' Janice said half an hour later as she finished emptying the picnic basket. ''But don't put off your walk any longer. I'm almost finished for tonight, anyway. Would you like your hair braided before you go out?"

Abbey handed her the comb.

"You know," Janice said with a glance at the many cabinets, "This kitchen is so overwhelming I think I'll just pack up the pots and pans I'll want at the cabin and give the rest to charity. It would make one heck of a garage sale for a worthy organization, and they could have it right here."

Abbey smiled. "The truth is you can't quite give up the good causes altogether, can you, Mom?" She braced herself so Janice could keep the proper tension as she braided. "Aren't you going to miss the house?"

"Of course. It's been home for a long time. There." She fastened the end of the long braid. "Don't be out too late."

"It won't take long," Abbey said.

She didn't realize how true that was until she got to Flynn's apartment. Not a single sliver of light was visible in the windows. On the off chance he had been painting and had simply forgotten that dusk was falling, she climbed the stairs and rapped on the door. But there was no answer, and finally she gave up.

She told herself she'd have another chance tomorrow. But there was a nasty little ache at the pit of her stomach. Dammit, she didn't want to put it off any longer. She wanted it all settled now.

Still, there wasn't much she could do about it as long as she didn't even know where the man was. She was on her way home when she met Boyd.

He saw her first and came hurrying up the path. "Your mother told me you were taking a walk," he said.

She nodded absently.

He dropped into step beside her. "Look, Abbey, I'm awfully sorry for what I said Friday, about Flynn and all."

He sounded very earnest, Abbey noticed. Well, perhaps she should give him the benefit of the doubt. She'd been rather hasty herself on Friday afternoon. "I think we were both a little short-tempered."

He seemed to relax. "I'm glad I caught you."

At least it was nice someone wanted to see her, Abbey thought. "Feel like a walk through the park?"

"Sure. It's the only chance I'll have to see you all week," Boyd said as they crossed Armitage Road.

"The firm is so busy?"

"One of the senior partners will be doing some serious negotiations in New York City this week, and he's taking me along to assist. Sort of on-the-job training. He obviously thinks I'm getting ready for great things."

"That's nice, Boyd."

"But next weekend when I'm back, we can spend some time together...."

Abbey shook her head. "It's Art on the Green."

"Oh, I'm planning on seeing that. We can go together."

"I'm afraid I'll be pretty busy. I volunteered to help run it."

Boyd frowned. "That means you'll be tied up with Flynn again, I suppose?"

Abbey stopped and looked levelly at him, eyebrows raised. "I thought you weren't going to make any more comments about Flynn."

"Oh, I understand what you're going through, Abbey," he said hastily. "I know you have to put a good face on this whole thing for your mother's sake right now, and if that means putting up with Flynn—"

A shout from across the park interrupted.

"Abbey! I need to talk to you!"

It was Sara Merrill's voice, but it took Abbey a moment to find her. Then she spotted a uniformed figure waving from the nearby softball field.

"It's about Art on the Green, I'm sure," Abbey said, "and it can't take long if Sara thinks she can fit it into the middle of a game."

"Of course I don't mind. I like the Merrills. His family gave the college Ashton Court and everything, you know."

"I know," Abbey said dryly.

"Oh, of course you would." Boyd grinned sheepishly. "I almost forgot you've spent most of your life here."

Sara had gone up to bat by the time they reached the field, so they sat down in the first row of bleachers by the dugout to wait for her return.

The game was between two teams sponsored by local businesses, and it was more enthusiastic than skilled. The crowd in the stands was hardly larger than that on the field, but it, too, was zealous.

Boyd said earnestly, "About Flynn, though. I know you can't do anything but tolerate him right now. And I've always said I can put up with anyone if there's an end in sight. Even Flynn Granger."

Abbey's jaw tightened. What a very generous stand, she thought sarcastically. The Merrills were lovely people, were they? And Flynn was nothing but dirt under Boyd's feet. Well, the only difference she could see was money—

Sara's bat cracked against the softball, and the crowd started to yell. One voice rang out above the others, or at least to Abbey's ears it seemed that way. One very familiar voice.

She turned to look up into the stands, and saw Flynn, three rows behind her and a little to one side, yelling his heart out as if he didn't have a care in the world.

It was then she realized that though she was disgusted by Boyd's hypocrisy, she wasn't hurt because her illusions about *him* had been fractured. The ache she was feeling was for Flynn. She couldn't stand the thought that someone—anyone!—was looking down his nose at Flynn.

Flynn, who had the gift of genius when he had a paintbrush in his hand. Flynn, who had the self-possession not to care about the status symbols the rest of the world found important.

Flynn, who had become so incredibly important to Abbey that she had been driving herself crazy wondering how to get things patched up between them. And who so obviously didn't give a hoot about whether the situation ever got back to normal.

CHAPTER NINE

ABBEY FORCED HERSELF to take a deep breath. Even if he had seen her, this was hardly the time or the place for a heart-to-heart chat: she was enjoying the ball game, so why should she be surprised that he was doing the same? Had she honestly expected Flynn to be huddled in a corner somewhere regretting that he'd told her off?

Not Flynn, she thought. He'd said what he believed, and he would stand by it. As far as he was concerned, that was the end of it....

Her throat was dry at the very thought. The end of what? she wondered. Of his respect for her? His liking for her? The friendship they'd been building?

Or had there been something even more important, tentatively growing between them, until she had accidentally put a screeching halt to it with her immature foolishness?

And why was it so important to her, anyway? Yes, she liked the man. She enjoyed the time she'd shared with him. The hours she spent in Flynn's company seemed to fly....

She admired his work; she could drown herself in the lustrous depths of his watercolors and not even notice how long she had silently sat and watched him paint, until her stiff muscles screamed in protest because she had forgotten to move.

And of course there was the way she reacted whenever he kissed her. She'd always had her fair share of attractive men hanging around, but she'd never had any trouble keeping things in perspective until Flynn had come along. But now...

Now, she admitted, she was having a great deal of trouble.

She told herself firmly not to be ridiculous, but it didn't help much. Once the suspicion was admitted it was impossible to root out again. She could very easily learn to care a great deal for Flynn.

No other flirtation had ever held quite the same edge, the same excitement, the same fun that she'd had with Flynn over the past few weeks. And yet, as contradictory as it sounded, she'd never been quite so much at ease with any other man, either. There were no awkward gaps to fill in conversation; it was comfortable simply to be silent with him, too.

"Don't take Flynn seriously," Sara had warned her just a couple of days before. "He's not the settling-down sort."

Abbey had laughed at the idea. Now it was no longer humorous, for she suddenly knew that she would like to take Flynn very seriously indeed.

He's like the other half of me. And if I could only believe that someday he might feel the same way...

A yell arose from the crowd. There was something about it that was more than the usual roar of excitement, and Abbey jerked out of her reverie. "What happened?" she asked, reaching out to Boyd as he jumped to his feet.

People from the field and from the stands were converging at second base around a figure sprawled on the ground. For a moment Abbey couldn't see who it was, but then the scene shifted a bit and she spotted long blond hair spread across the dust. Whatever sort of spill had put Sara on the ground had been powerful enough to knock her hat off.

"Your friend Sara collided with the shortstop." Boyd was leaning into the dugout fence to get the best possible view.

"I'm going down to help," Abbey said.

"There are plenty of people already on the field," Boyd pointed out. "I don't know what you could accomplish except to get in the way."

"Neither do I, but I certainly can't do any good from here."

Sara was sitting up by the time they reached the field, but her face was white and pasty. She managed a smile. "It's all right. A few weeks in a cast will give me a vacation." She grimaced as the team's manager slipped an inflatable splint over her calf. She looked up and met Abbey's eyes. "I don't suppose you'd like to take over Art on the Green altogether? This is going to put a serious crimp in my style."

"Of course I will," Abbey said.

"Don't worry about it now, Sara," Flynn said. "Everything will get done—I'll see to it."

Abbey watched as Sara's stretcher was carried off, and then her gaze sought out Flynn across the circle. He hadn't needed to make it sound as if she couldn't be counted on at all. Her jaw tightened in frustration.

That was exactly what he thought, she realized. And she had given him every reason to think that way.

Tears stung her eyelids. "Dammit, Flynn..."

He swung around to face her, one eyebrow raised.

Not exactly a good way to start an abject apology, she reminded herself. But then, this wasn't exactly the moment for it, either. If she was specific, with this crowd milling about, she would only make things worse by repeating the insult. And if she didn't say precisely what she meant, goodness only knew what kind of a story would fly around town. No, making her amends would have to wait.

"I'll take care of Art on the Green," she said.

"I'm glad to hear it." He strode off the field after the stretcher.

She watched him go and tried to swallow the panicky sensation that she had lost something that could never be retrieved. She shouldn't feel hopeless, and helpless, and alone, she told herself. The timing had been all wrong, but that wasn't her fault. It didn't mean there wouldn't be another opportunity to correct things. After all, even Boyd understood they couldn't simply avoid each other.

She would do the best she could with Art on the Green, and when she had a real chance, she would tell Flynn she was sorry for what she had said. And then perhaps he would stop looking at her as he had just now—as a brother would, obviously seeing a nuisance of a little sister who every so often needed to be straightened out.

She'd once said that Flynn was the last person on earth she would want as a brother, and she'd been absolutely correct. The problem was that all the reasons she had given herself had been the wrong ones.

THE STAFFORD HOUSE was beginning to smell like a restaurant from early morning till late at night as Norma mass-produced hors d'oeuvres to be frozen until the wedding reception. The oven timer was already buzzing as Abbey came down the stairs, still yawning. She took one look at Norma, up to her elbows in dough, and rescued the pan of tiny pizzas from the heat. Then Abbey glanced over the huge array of edibles and picked up a sausage wrapped in a blanket of evenly browned pastry. Norma slapped at her hand and flour flew everywhere.

Abbey dropped the sausage. "But you've made thousands," she protested. "And the caterer will be bringing thousands more."

Norma snorted. "Plastic snacks, that's what the caterer's bringing. What would there be to eat if I didn't make some real food?"

"But can't you spare one sausage? Call it my breakfast."

"You wouldn't stop with one. Don't you want to fit into your dress for the wedding?"

Abbey reached for a freezer container and started to layer sausage rolls into it. "If I say no, does that mean I can eat my share of the hors d'oeuvres right now?" She was toying with the image of herself as a blimp, too large to fit into the softly draped ice-green dress Janice had chosen for her, and therefore unable to take her part in the ceremony. But of course it wasn't the idea of witnessing her mother's wedding vows that was bothering her these days. It was the fact that she would be sharing that job with Flynn, who was to be his father's best man.

Norma watched her suspiciously as if expecting another raid on the food. "That Boyd Baxter wouldn't like the idea of your getting fat, I'll bet." She started to knead another batch of dough. "He called again last night. That's three times this week."

Abbey nodded. "I saw your note." She snapped the top on the freezer container and reached for another one.

"He asked where you were. I told him you were working on Art on the Green. He said he'd be back in town tomorrow."

"Great. That's just what I need." Abbey sounded absentmindedly; her thoughts were on the mass of instructions Sara had passed on last night. If she managed to get through the weekend without messing up, it would be a miracle.

"What are you two discussing?" Janice came in, dressed in a casual divided skirt and a tailored blouse.

"Boyd Baxter," Norma said.

Janice looked at her wristwatch, poured herself precisely half a cup of coffee and leaned against the dishwasher. "I'll be glad when all this fuss is over and I can relax. What about Boyd, anyway?"

Norma sniffed. "He reminds me of Mr. Stafford, that's all."

"What a nice compliment for Boyd," Abbey murmured.

The housekeeper shot a look at her. "I didn't exactly mean it that way."

Abbey wasn't listening. "My goodness, look here. One of your sausages got twisted somewhere along the line, Norma. We can't put that out on the bridal buffet and ruin your reputation for creating perfect food, can we?" She grinned, popped the tidbit into her mouth and chewed appreciatively.

Janice rinsed her cup and set it aside. "If you're going up to Chandler this morning, I'll drop you off, Abbey."

Abbey thought she might as well accept the offer. In the past four days, she had walked past Flora Pembroke's house a dozen times, and she hadn't seen Flynn outside even once. The odds of him being in sight this morning were no better.

This couldn't go on. She had to run into him somewhere soon—at Art on the Green this weekend if not before. Of course, she could make another stab at purposely tracking him down, but something deep inside made her shudder away from that idea. A casual apology was one thing, but making a special effort to see him would make it all seem too important somehow. And after the way he had looked at her there on the softball field, she couldn't bear it if—

"Did you hear me?" Janice asked.

Abbey blinked. "Just let me grab my briefcase."

As Janice started the car, Abbey said, "I feel guilty, walking out on Norma when she's knee-deep in food like that."

"For heaven's sake, don't volunteer to help! If she had two more hands, she'd just extend the list of things to make." Janice sighed. "It would have been easier to have a civil ceremony in the courthouse and skip the festivities altogether. It's not the wedding that matters, after all—it's the marriage. All that's really necessary is two people who care about each other."

There was a note of soft certainty in her voice that made Abbey's throat tighten in wistful longing. Two people, she thought, who loved each other; that was all. But if either of them didn't feel that way. . .

"You told me about the table collapsing," Abbey said abruptly, "and that you knew then you really cared about Frank. But how did it start? How did you fall in love?"

Janice shot a look of astonishment at her, and Abbey realized it must be the first time she had ever admitted that what her mother felt for Frank was really love, and not some illusion of second childhood.

Janice smiled softly. "I suppose it really started the day he installed the new disposal in the kitchen. You know how we always want exactly what we can't have?"

That had a familiar ring to it, Abbey thought.

"There was no water, and I was perishing for a cup of coffee. So Frank offered me a cup from his thermos, and we sat and talked for a while...." Janice's voice trailed off. Her face had turned slightly pink, and her eyes were dreamy.

Abbey almost said, "How romantic," but she stopped her sarcastic comment just in time. If their roles had been reversed, and she had been asked when she had first found herself attracted to Flynn, what would she have said? When she'd first seen his work hanging at Ashton Court? When she'd found him trimming roses in Flora Pembroke's garden, hot and bare-chested and altogether appealing? Or even longer ago, back in their school years, when once in a while his caricatures had targeted her?

"I think if I hadn't made the first move, though," Janice reflected, "I'd probably be on my way to the garden club this morning, instead of to the dressmaker. You did say you're going up to Chandler?"

"Yes, but the library isn't open yet." Abbey looked around and made a quick decision. "Drop me off at the cemetery instead, would you?"

Quick concern sprang to life in Janice's eyes.

Abbey answered the unspoken question. "I'm not brooding, Mom. I'm perfectly fine."

Janice didn't say any more, but her parting smile couldn't hide a trace of worry.

It was a beautiful June morning, but the air held a promise of oppressive warmth to come before the day was much older. By the time Abbey reached the top of the hill she was wishing she had left her briefcase at home.

The fresh lilacs she had put on her father's grave were long ago faded and gone, and she had replaced them with an arrangement of silk flowers that would last through the summer. But the bouquet was not the only new decoration on Warren Stafford's grave. Near the big granite headstone with its deep-carved letters was a small bush with glossy heart-shaped leaves. There was, of course, no sign of flowers. But in springs to come, Abbey knew, there would be masses of purple blossoms scenting the air across the hill.

"A lilac," Abbey whispered, and sank down on the grass to stare at it.

Seeing the simple little bush helped heal her heart in a way no grander gesture could possibly have. Warren Stafford's house would leave the family, and his precious row of lilacs might even be cut down to make a different sort of garden. But those things weren't important, as long as Warren was remembered—not as a saint, not as a villain, but as the brilliant and forceful man he had been.

And when Abbey left the cemetery a little later, her step was light and her briefcase seemed to weigh hardly anything at all.

ABBEY HEARD THE WHINE of the electric sander as she approached the Campbells' patio, and she was less than ten feet from Frank by the time he saw her. "Good afternoon, Abbey," he said, and turned away to pick up his tape measure.

"What are you building?"

"Bookcases. Building them outside saves Mrs. Campbell a bit of sawdust and lets me get some fresh air." He consulted a sketch and pulled a pencil out of his pocket to mark a board.

What was it Janice had told her this morning? If she hadn't made the first move, everything would still be just the same—that was it. And what about Abbey? Unless she made that first move, would her relationship with Frank always be like this—quiet and polite, but never quite friendly?

"Mind if I sit and talk a minute?" she asked.

Frank looked up from his board. The tilt of his eyebrows reminded her uncomfortably of Flynn. "Not at all."

She watched him, his hands moving surely against the smooth wood, and deep inside her something stirred, a long-forgotten memory of another time when she had watched him work in total silence. "Remember the day you fixed my bike?" she asked.

Frank smiled a little. "I sure do."

"I must have been eight or nine," she mused. "I was late for dinner, and I wasn't where I was supposed to be, and the chain slipped off. I must have been a mile from home.... Did you know I didn't have permission to be off Armitage Road?"

He nodded.

"But you never said a word. You put the chain back on, and you loaded me and the bike into your truck and hauled me all the way home...."

"Not quite all the way."

Abbey snapped her fingers. "That's why you stopped up by the Pembrokes', so I wouldn't get into trouble. Why didn't you tell me? I was so afraid you'd talk to my father, it kept me straight for a year."

"I thought it might," Frank said soberly.

"It's not that I was afraid of him, exactly. I don't think he ever spanked me, but he had such a way of making me feel bad when I'd misbehaved that I'd do anything to avoid it."

She pulled her heels up on the edge of the patio bench and hugged her knees, waiting to see if Frank would jump on this opportunity to discuss Warren Stafford's failings.

But he didn't say a word. He just looked at her with compassion in those clear blue eyes.

Janice had told her once that she was a smart girl, so she ought to be able to look at Frank and see what attracted her mother. At the time, Abbey hadn't the vaguest idea what Janice was talking about, but now she knew. It was the peacefulness in his attitude, his essential gentleness.

He was easy to be with, easy to talk to. Abbey should certainly understand the attraction that quality held for Janice, since it was one of the things Abbey herself found so appealing about Flynn. There was a comforting quiet about both of them....

Except, of course, when Flynn was handing out lectures on Abbey's bad behavior.

And even then, she told herself, it wouldn't have been so awful if she'd thought he'd done it because he cared about her. But of course, it wasn't that at all. He had given her that dressing-down purely because she was being a nuisance to a couple of people he loved.

She sighed, admitting that perhaps she hadn't gone out of her way to face Flynn because she knew very well that no mere apology was going to smooth things over. It wasn't going to be easy to fix this one—if it was even possible.

But at least now she knew what she needed to do about Frank. No one, least of all Frank, expected her to put him in her father's place. But she could build him a spot of his own in her heart, and in her life.

She could not, however, bring herself to say anything quite so sentimental, even though she suspected it wouldn't fluster Frank at all. Instead, she simply smiled at him. "I was just up at the cemetery. Does Mother know about the lilac bush?"

"Now why would you ask me about that?"

"Because it's just the kind of wonderful thing you'd do."

His eyes began to twinkle. "Yes, she knows. We did it together—a lilac for your dad, and a rhododendron for my Kitty."

She remembered the Sunday they had gone out to visit the cemeteries. "I'm glad," Abbey whispered. She sat there quietly for a little while longer, watching his hands shape the wood moldings that would trim the Campbells' bookcase. "I'd better get going. I've got work to do."

"How's the dissertation coming along?"

She made a face. "Slowly. And there's no progress on a job at the moment, either. I've got all kinds of applications out, though, and I should be hearing about interviews soon, so you don't need to worry about my hanging around under your roof forever."

"It wasn't keeping me up nights," Frank murmured.

"That's very sweet of you. Especially since it can't quite be the truth, considering the way I've been behaving. Oh, and Frank—" she turned at the edge of the patio "—if you happen to have another of those nice carved jewelry boxes lying about somewhere..."

It was the first time she had really seen him smile, and the change it made in him startled her. If that was how he looked at Janice when they were alone, Abbey thought, it explained a lot of things.

I couldn't ask for anything more myself than that sort of look in a man's eyes. The eyes of the man I love...

She told herself bluntly not to count on seeing it. Flynn might have inherited his self-sufficient attitude from his father, and his confidence, and even that essential gentleness. But it certainly didn't mean he'd also acquired Frank's fondness for the Stafford women.

At least, she thought, not for both of the Stafford women.

THE ART FAIR was slated to open at ten in the morning, but there were people roaming the block-long stretch of Chandler's commons even before the last of the booths were set up. And by nine-thirty, Abbey was starting to tear out her hair because only a fraction of Sara's volunteers had arrived.

At a booth near the front gate, Flynn was hanging watercolors on the display boards. "Don't panic," he said. "It's always like this right before opening."

It was the first time they'd been within speaking distance all morning, and his tone of voice was absolutely neutral—as if he didn't even remember their quarrel. Abbey wasn't sure whether to be grateful or annoyed.

"Just a minute and I'll give you a hand," he added.

Abbey looked over her shoulder at his booth. "Thanks, but it looks to me as if you have plenty to do." She swallowed hard and forced herself to walk over to him. Despite the bedlam surrounding them, she'd better seize the opportunity if she intended to talk to him today. Once the gates officially opened it wasn't going to get any easier.

The watercolor he was hanging was the dark rich scene of the train beside the Victorian depot, and Abbey looked at it longingly, remembering the afternoon she'd sat quietly in the wing chair and watched as he painted it. She must have been falling in love with him even then, she thought.

She didn't bother to check the price tag discreetly attached to the corner of the frame; until she had some sort of job, her bank account was certainly not in the condition to be buying luxuries.

"Yes?" Flynn said.

Abbey jumped. "I just wanted to tell you that I'm awfully sorry for what I said that afternoon on the tree."

He didn't answer, just looked down at her thoughtfully. His eyes seemed to have taken on even more of a slant.

Her voice shook a little, despite her best efforts to keep it steady. "You were entirely right about Frank and Mother, and I..." She saw a group of people bearing down on the entrance gate and added gratefully, "I have to go now."

She handed out programs and tried to ignore the fact that Flynn was still leaning against the side of his booth and watching her with what could only be suspicion.

You certainly blew that, Abbey told herself.

She should have treated the episode casually, as just another minor matter that needed clearing up. Instead, she'd been so nervous and anxious that she'd practically invited him to wonder why the whole thing should be so blessed important to her.

Boyd appeared at the gate. Abbey greeted him with relief and thrust a pile of programs into his hand. "Here," she ordered. "Make sure everyone who comes in gets one of these. There will be someone along to spell you whenever I can shanghai a warm body."

"But I came to..." Boyd's protest trailed off helplessly as Abbey turned away into the crowd.

"What great planning, Boyd," she heard Flynn say. "You'll certainly get to meet all the art patrons in town from there."

Abbey spotted a stray volunteer three booths down and started after her.

Running away was no permanent solution of course, and she knew it. Sooner or later, Flynn would begin to suspect what was really going on.

And that she couldn't bear. Having to face him at every holiday, every family event, would be bad enough. But knowing he understood how she felt about him—and that he was sorry for her—would be infinitely worse.

There was only one way out of this, she decided. Somehow she had to get back to the old easy habit of flirting and fun and careless humor, so he didn't suspect that anything had changed at all.

"I never realized before what a wonderful experience this is," Sara Merrill mused an hour or so later.

Her voice was at the level of Abbey's elbow, and Abbey jumped and wheeled around, startled to see Sara in a wheelchair. Her leg cast, already decorated from hip to toe in a garish rainbow, stuck out in front of her like a battering ram.

"The show, I mean, not the cast and the wheelchair," Sara went on. "Though perhaps next year we should roll the lawn to level it. Funny how I never thought of that before all the bumps started rattling my spine. Is the judging already done?"

Abbey snapped her fingers. "I forgot all about that. Where's the judge, anyway?" She looked around almost wildly for the visiting art professor who was to name the best entries.

By the time she caught up with him, he had visited nearly all the booths, and Abbey let out a sigh of relief as she realized how little she had been missed. Perhaps, she thought, he preferred to work by himself, even though Sara had warned her she should expect to be assistant judge, secretary or even a stand-in easel if the professor needed a painting held up for comparison.

But she was not to be so fortunate. "Now that you're here, we can start some serious work," the professor said coolly.

"I thought you'd seen everything already."

"You wouldn't expect me to start hanging ribbons on some things before I've seen them all, would you? Now I'll go back for a closer inspection." He thrust a clipboard at her. "You can take notes."

In a booth full of ceramic sculpture, as the professor took his time over an elaborate grinning dragon, Dave Talbot came up to Abbey.

"You haven't stopped by my office for our talk," he accused.

"I'm sorry, Dave. I just haven't had the opportunity." She kept one eye on the professor as he picked up the dragon and studied the artist's marks on the base.

"I've found a job for you."

The professor was forgotten. "Where?" Abbey said eagerly. "Doing what?"

Dave Talbot's eyebrows raised. "I had no idea you were desperate. Here at Chandler, teaching English literature."

"I thought you didn't have any vacancies."

"That was before Sara broke her leg."

Abbey's initial excitement faded away. "Oh, you mean just to fill in for the summer sessions till she's out of the cast?"

"No, she only has one seminar right now and it's being covered by another staff member. But she's decided to take a leave of absence starting in the fall. It might be only a one-year contract, Abbey, but—"

The professor said firmly, "I'm ready to move on now, Miss Stafford."

"Come and talk to me next week about the curriculum," Dave Talbot said. "See if you're interested." He picked up a ceramic candlestick and pulled out his wallet.

It might be only for one year, Abbey reminded herself as they worked their way through the next couple of booths. But so far nothing else looked promising. This would fill the gap that was beginning to yawn in front of her and give her time to look for another post. If she didn't take this opportunity, and none of her other applications bore fruit, she would have to look for another sort of job. At least this position was in her field. A year at Chandler would look good on her résumé and would mean she wouldn't have to depend on Janice and Frank for a place to live....

"...in the log cabin," she said aloud.

"What was that?" the professor demanded. "The log cabin, did you say? No, Miss Stafford. I very clearly told you the depot and the train. The one called *At the Station.*"

Abbey looked up in astonishment at a very familiar watercolor. She had been so preoccupied with Dave Talbot's offer she hadn't even noticed they were back at the first booth—Flynn's booth.

The professor jabbed his finger at the dark cloud rising from the steam engine's funnels. "Best of show, I said, because of the density of the smoke and the lustrous play of light on the bricks."

It was no surprise. Abbey had certainly seen nothing here today that could measure up to Flynn's work. But wasn't it just her luck that the moment she had a job offer and could have bought the painting, it was snatched out of her reach?

She sighed and checked her notes for the amount of the prize. "Best of show is the Reynolds purchase award," she said. "Five thousand dollars and purchase price to the artist, and the painting goes to Chandler College to hang in Ashton Court." Right beside last year's winner.

Flynn's client, a redhead who had been admiring a painting at the back of the booth, went on to the next display. Flynn crossed to the corner where Abbey and the professor stood.

"Congratulations," the professor announced grandly, thrusting out his hand. "You have a future, young man."

Flynn brushed the praise aside. "You're talking about *At the Station*? I really didn't intend to let that go today."

Abbey's pen stopped in midword. She peered at the tag on the corner of the frame. "But you've listed a price."

She glanced at the nearby paintings and frowned. *At the Station* was undoubtedly the best thing in the booth, but why had he priced it at more than double what his other work sold for?

"And what a price, too," she muttered. "If you're holding it back to give it to Frank and Mother as a wedding gift, you should have marked it Not for Sale."

"I'm not planning to give it to them."

"I don't see why you put a price on it at all if you don't want to sell it."

"I didn't say I wouldn't. But I'm not in any hurry, so I thought I'd start high and let negotiations determine the real value."

Abbey shrugged. "I'd think you'd drive customers away. I'd be interested myself at a reasonable amount, but—"

Flynn's eyebrows raised. "Yes? And what do you think is reasonable, Abbey?"

She was tongue-tied, stuck in a dilemma of her own making. If she told him what she could afford to pay, she'd be insulting the quality of his work. But if she gave the figure she honestly thought was right and he agreed to sell it to her, she'd have to arrange a payment plan....

"Abbey?"

Abbey's pulse was fluttering and her throat was dry. *Would* he sell it to her? Was it possible that he might *want* her to have it?

No, she thought. It was only wishful thinking again. He understood precisely the spot she had put herself in and he was enjoying it. That was all.

She had decided an hour ago that she had to get things back to normal. Well, she told herself, this was the best chance she was ever going to have to accomplish that.

She raised her chin and said teasingly, "I don't have that much cash. I'm afraid you'd have to agree to take my body in trade."

A wicked sparkle sprang to life in Flynn's eyes. He pulled up a high stool and perched on the edge of the seat with his arms folded across his chest. "In that case," he murmured, "I'll hold out for the whole five thousand dollars' worth."

And what a flaming public affair that would be. She smiled. "Take the prize money, Flynn. Besides, think of the honor."

"I was," he said. His voice was soft, almost silky.

"Best of show," Abbey said firmly and wrote on the judge's sheet, *"At the Station,* by Flynn Granger."

For one long-drawn-out moment he was silent, and Abbey held her breath. If he really did want her to have the painting, instead of seeing it hang at Chandler College...

But the moment passed. Flynn shook his head and laughed, then accepted the professor's handshake and thanked him for the award and the compliment to his work.

It was a good thing she hadn't taken him seriously, Abbey thought. It would have been almighty embarrassing.

The professor took the clipboard and went off to give the good news to all the other winners. For a moment, Flynn and Abbey were alone in the corner of the booth.

"Congratulations," she said, and put her hand out to him. "Two years in a row. Has that ever happened before?"

He didn't release her; he simply folded her hand inside his own and kept it there.

"I'll ask Sara," Abbey said quickly. "She'll know."

"Only a handshake?" he whispered. "Nothing more?" Still holding her hand, he brushed the tip of his index finger across her lips. It was a sultry, suggestive gesture, and it made Abbey's heart pound with longing. Half the town might walk in at any moment, and she didn't care.

"Of course I can spare more than a handshake." She stood on tiptoe to press a long, firm kiss on the corner of his mouth. "Congratulations, Flynn. You deserve it."

She saw the bemused look in his eyes, and she had the comfort of knowing she'd succeeded. They were right back to where they'd started.

And that made her want to cry, because that wasn't where she wanted to be at all. She wanted so much more.

But what on earth could she do about it?

CHAPTER TEN

THERE WAS NO LONGER a steady stream of people coming through the entrance gates, but newcomers continued to trickle in. Boyd was standing faithfully at the gate fanning himself with a program. Whenever someone appeared he handed the program over, picked up the next one from his pile and started to fan again. He looked as if his feet hurt.

He saw Abbey coming and relief flickered in his eyes. "Can I leave now?" he asked almost plaintively.

Abbey had forgotten her promise to find someone to spell him. Not that it would have done much good even if she had remembered, since she hadn't had time to look for a replacement. "Just as soon as I find a volunteer, Boyd. Only a few minutes more..."

"That's what you said an hour ago," he grumbled. "I wouldn't mind seeing the displays myself, you know."

"Oh, don't worry about it," Flynn said. "Your timing is perfect. All the ribbons will be in place in another five minutes, so you won't even have to think about what to applaud. Do you want anything from the refreshment stand, Abbey?"

She shook her head. Flynn went off whistling, and Abbey looked around for anyone who might fill in. She'd do it herself except that as soon as she settled down at the gate she was certain to be needed elsewhere.

Less than ten yards away, Sara's wheelchair was at the center of a knot of people. She could surely hand out programs even while she was holding court, Abbey thought.

Sara saw her coming. "You're doing a great job, Abbey," she called. "Everyone's saying what a wonder you're to step in on such short notice. And I must say the sartorial quality of the volunteers has gone up immensely." She winked at Boyd.

"As long as I'm recruiting volunteers," Abbey said, "how about you?" She took the stack of programs from Boyd's hand and held them out to Sara.

"I'm a wounded woman," Sara complained. "You expect me to work?"

"You've still got hands. Anyway, this is just a last bit of duty before you leave all your responsibilities behind. You didn't tell me you were taking a leave of absence."

Sara's eyebrows drew together and she began to straighten the already neat stack of programs. "I wasn't keeping it secret. In fact, I told Dave Talbot you'd be perfect for the job. So when you didn't mention it last week, I thought..."

"That he hadn't offered it to me, after all?"

"Not exactly. I thought you'd turned it down." Sara's gaze slid to Flynn's booth nearby. "I didn't want to embarrass you."

It was no secret what Sara was thinking. "He just asked me," she said, and realized too late that the phrase could have more than one meaning, and this audience was likely to jump on the wrong one. "Dave, I mean. He offered me the job just a few minutes ago."

"You're taking it?" Sara asked.

"I'm not quite sure. I have to think about it."

Boyd put one arm around Abbey and planted a kis firmly on her cheek. "Of course you'll take it. This isn' just a summer romance, you know."

Something inside Abbey seemed to quick-freeze. She wasn't certain if it was because of the possessive wa Boyd had kissed her, or the fact that Flynn, on his way back from the concession stand with a soft drink, did double take.

"It isn't?" Flynn said. "But Boyd, I was so sure you' be heartbroken when Abbey left that I even recruite volunteers for a suicide watch."

It was apparent Flynn wasn't going to be heartbro ken, Abbey thought. The plain fact was that Flynn didn' really give a damn what she did or where she went.

She lifted her chin. "I'm going to check on the chi drens' activity booth. Are you coming, Boyd?"

She stepped away from his encircling arm and hurrie off down the green to the far end, where on a shade patch of lawn a half-dozen children were experimentin with finger paints. Here the busy bustle of the festival wa subdued. Except for the excited noise of the children, i was practically peaceful.

Boyd said contentedly, "Everything does have a wa of working out, doesn't it? Not that we need any mor time. I have absolutely no doubts."

"Neither have I," Abbey said.

Boyd beamed.

"You're absolutely right, Boyd. We're not having summer romance. In fact, we're not having any sort o romance at all, and we're not ever likely to. So you ca stop assuming that all you have to do is ask and I'll marr you."

Boyd said stiffly, "This is not an appropriate topic fo a public place."

"You're the one who brought it up back at the gate. You should be grateful I didn't straighten you out right there, Boyd."

His face had gone dull red. "The company you've been keeping has had a very bad influence on you, Abbey."

"I know," she said sweetly. "Aren't you lucky to escape?"

FLYNN WAS IN AND OUT of the Stafford house almost every day during the week before the wedding. He was running errands for Janice, and he didn't seem to notice whether or not he saw Abbey. If she were there, he flirted or pressed her into helping. If she weren't, he simply did the job and went away.

She never knew when to expect him, either, and so she didn't even have the comfort of being able to prepare herself. It was like living on the edge of a cliff, never quite sure when a gust of wind would sweep her over. Gone was the old peaceful ease of being in his company, and every time she saw him, Abbey told herself it would be a whole lot better to stay completely away.

Yet even when she had a good excuse to avoid him, there was something magnetic about his presence. If she so much as heard his voice, Abbey's own work suddenly lost its attraction and she instantly felt an overwhelming need to get something from whichever room he was in.

Two days before the wedding, she actually found herself dumping an entire soda down the drain in her bathroom just so she could take the empty can to the kitchen where he was and innocently reach for a fresh one.

"You're crazy, girl," she muttered. But she went downstairs, anyway.

Flynn was sitting at the breakfast bar sampling hors d'oeuvres. Abbey eyed the array in front of him and asked, "How did you manage to wheedle Norma into that?"

Flynn flexed his biceps. "I moved the dining-room table." He munched a tiny pizza round.

"That's it? I've been scrubbing this place from top to bottom and all she'll let me have is crackers and diet soda."

He picked up a shrimp puff and studied it with a philosophical air. "What's it worth to you for me to share?"

Abbey's adrenaline level increased a fraction. "What have you got in mind?" she countered.

"I need help."

For a change he sounded serious. Abbey popped the top on her soda can. "What kind of help?"

"Flowers. I haven't any idea what kind of bridal bouquet Janice would like. And I don't want to ask Janice, because she shouldn't have to choose it herself; it's the groom's responsibility."

"And the groom passed the job off to you?"

"He seems to think I've got lots of experience."

Abbey smiled. "With bridal bouquets? He can't have been thinking clearly, can he? Now if he just needed the odd rosebud clipped from the bush or a bunch of forget-me-nots, I'm sure you'd be—"

"Abbey, would you just come with me to see the florist? I'll admit I owe you a favor in return. Anything you want, kid."

Anything at all, she thought, except what she'd really like to have—because favors don't extend to falling in love.

But she kept her voice light and playful. "Certainly, dear boy. You can start by handing over a shrimp puff."

He did better than that; he fed it to her. As she bit into the pastry shell, part of the rich filling oozed over his fingertips, and he automatically raised them to his mouth.

"Not on your life," Abbey said, her mouth still full. "That's mine." Her hand closed around his wrist to hold it steady, and she began to lick each fingertip clean.

The sensation was more sensual than she had bargained for, but there was no graceful way to stop. The light saltiness of his skin mingled with the rich flavor of shrimp, and the warmth of his fingers against her tongue made her want to close her eyes and just keep on tasting him. She was feeling very unsteady inside by the time she released her hold.

Flynn looked at his hand as if he half expected to find a finger or two missing. "Are you sure you got it all?"

"Just like eating a Popsicle." Abbey congratulated herself. Her voice was a shade lower than usual, but otherwise she sounded perfectly normal. "Only the wooden sticks left. Now didn't you say something about flowers?"

IN THE END, not even the weather stood in the way of Janice's wedding. The ceremony was to be at eleven in the garden behind the Stafford house, and the morning dawned clear and sunny with a light breeze and not so much as a drop of dew.

At nine, still wearing the shorts and T-shirt she had pulled on when she got out of bed, Abbey was helping Norma arrange trays of hors d'oeuvres and trying to convince her to leave room on the buffet table for the items the caterer was bringing.

At ten, Janice came home from the hairdresser, looking as coolly elegant as any bride could wish, and said, 'Didn't the lawn service show up this morning? I think a dead limb has fallen out of the oak tree at the back of the garden, and it's lying right across the clearing.''

''I told you to get that tree cut down,'' Norma grumbled.

Janice looked puzzled. ''Is it dead? Well, I'll just go drag the branch off myself. There isn't time to call the lawn people now.''

Abbey set down a tray of tiny ham and cheese pinwheels. ''I'll take care of it, Mom.''

''But you have to get dressed, Abbey.''

''So do you. And nobody's going to be looking at me.'' At least, she devoutly hoped no one would be paying attention to the bride's daughter today. ''Besides,'' she murmured, ''the caterer's trucks just pulled in, and someone is going to have to keep Norma in hand. Frankly, I'd rather deal with the branch, because it won't argue.''

The breeze in the garden felt cool against her flushed cheeks. It would be nice, Abbey thought, to be able to slow down and enjoy this day. Perhaps Janice had been right; a quiet little civil ceremony sounded like a delightful idea.

The limb was a big one, and it had fallen directly in the middle of the small glade where the ceremony was to be held. Abbey was debating how to get the best possible leverage, and so she didn't hear soft footsteps on the path at the edge of the garden or see Flynn as he came toward her.

''Good morning,'' he said.

Abbey jumped and lost her grip. The branch she had been holding slashed at her, and she leapt back and swore. ''You're a lot of help,'' she accused.

"If I'd known I was needed, I'd have been here sooner," Flynn said mildly. "Where are we taking this, anyway?"

He was already dressed for the wedding in a pearl-gray suit with a white shirt and a softy patterned tie. The pale colors made his eyes look bigger and a darker blue than Abbey had ever seen them before, and she had to swallow hard against the surge of longing that rose from the pit of her stomach. If she only had the freedom to walk up to him, lay her fingertips gently on his lapels, stare up into his eyes and drown herself in the mystery of them....

He raised a hand to straighten his tie, and her eyes widened when she saw the pristine white bandage wrapped around his fingers.

She gasped. "That's your painting hand, Flynn! What did you do to it?"

He glanced at the white gauze. "Oh, I was pulling weeds in Flora's garden. It's been so dry that everything's rooted deeper than usual, and I was tugging so hard I broke a blood vessel in my finger."

"Taking risks like that with your hands... Flynn, you idiot!"

"It's just a bruise, not serious at all. The bandage is really only there to remind me not to move too fast. Shall we stash the limb in those bushes for now?"

There was a secluded little corner behind the row of boxwood sheltered by the remaining oak trees. A few stray shafts of sunlight found their way through the maze of branches and dappled the moss-covered ground. The hidden spot was quiet and isolated. It would have been a beautiful place to slip away and steal a kiss....

And why not? Abbey asked herself. Even if it didn't mean anything at all, why shouldn't she kiss him if she wanted? Or even have an affair—not the flaming public sort he had talked of originally, of course, but some thing private and intense and very passionate, for as long as both of them wanted it to continue?

As if he had read her mind, Flynn's arm came around her very gently. Abbey's eyes closed and she snuggled against him with a little sound that was more whimper than sigh. And when his mouth brushed hers, she kissed him back with every ounce of feeling she possessed.

He was obviously startled at the extent of her response, but even then he did not demand surrender or try to overwhelm her. He did not need force, or anything like it. *He will never hurt me,* she was thinking. *That essential gentleness in him means I don't have to be afraid...*

No, she realized. It only meant he would never deliberately harm her. But Flynn had no idea how very vulnerable she was, and how easy it would be to break her like a plastic toy. So long as this was, for him, only a new sort of game, Abbey would never be quite secure. She would never be safe.

She pushed herself away from him with a jerk. ''I'd better go and get dressed,'' she said almost hoarsely, and turned toward the house.

''Abbey...''

She stopped in midstep, her back to him. ''I'm sorry. That was a mistake.''

Flynn moved up behind her; his hands came to rest on her shoulders.

The backs of Abbey's eyelids began to prickle a bit. ''I still have to shower and dress and do my hair and makeup.''

His fingers began to move, massaging her tense muscles in an almost hypnotic rhythm.

Abbey could hear voices in the garden, soft murmurs coming closer with each passing minute. ''Look,'' she said desperately. "The guests are starting to arrive, and I'll never be ready on time."

"Then we'll take this up later," Flynn whispered. "You can count on it."

"It was a mistake, Flynn."

He gave her a tiny push. "Go."

Abbey ducked through the boxwood, circled the clearing and was completely breathless by the time she got to the house.

It's all right, she told herself. *I've got till after the wedding to pull myself together and decide how to explain that momentary aberration.*

The speed she achieved in getting dressed was likely to stand in the record books for all time when it came to maids of honor. Abbey supposed she only managed the feat because she would have welcomed anything to delay the wedding's start—a run in her panty hose, a mascara wand stuck in her eye, a French twist that simply would not stay in place. But none of those things happened. At precisely five minutes to the hour, when Janice knocked on her door, Abbey was ready.

Janice was wearing a soft off-white linen suit with a blouse the same shade of icy green as Abbey's dress and a tiny hat that perched at an angle above one ear. She peered at herself in the mirror and then turned to straighten the spray of exotic lilies tucked in Abbey's hair. Her fingers were shaking.

Abbey smoothed her skirt and checked the hemline in the mirror. "Let's go," she said.

Down in the kitchen, the clergyman was looking out the long windows at the back of the house, peering at the waiting crowd to see if everyone was in place. Frank was pacing the floor; he stopped abruptly as they came in. Flynn was just biting into a bacon-wrapped mushroom.

His eyes took on a contented gleam, and Abbey felt soft heat wash over her.

It's probably just the mushroom he's so happy with, she told herself briskly. *And if I can just keep on thinking that...*

Flynn took two large white boxes from the refrigerator. In one lay a spray of exotic lilies that matched the ones in Abbey's hair, three perfect blooms tied with streamers of dark green ribbon. She looked down at them, focusing on the small drops of water that clung to the waxy petals, because she didn't dare meet his eyes.

Janice had laid both hands on Frank's lapels and was looking up at him with a tremulous smile.

"Any doubts?" he said softly, and she shook her head.

"I should hope not," Flynn said. "After all the trouble I took over the flowers, you wouldn't dare—"

"The trouble *you* took?" Abbey sputtered. "You'd have come out of there with sweetheart roses and baby's breath. You're a fraud, Flynn Granger."

There was a gleam of unholy amusement in his eyes as he unwrapped Janice's nosegay of white lilies, his fingers a bit awkward because of the bandage on his hand, and presented it to her with a courtly bow.

The clergyman cleared his throat and asked, "Are we all ready?" He led the way out to the patio without waiting for an answer.

"I think he's afraid the whole thing will disintegrate into chaos," Flynn murmured. He offered his arm.

Abbey allowed only her fingertips to brush his sleeve. "I can't see why." Her voice dripped irony. "The simple fact that you're involved..."

They crossed the drive and went up the flagstone steps into the garden. "Janice told me Boyd sent his regrets," Flynn said under his breath. "And Norma said you weren't seeing him anymore. What really happened, anyway?''

Abbey was amazed at how cool her voice was. "If I'd known you were interested, I'd have given you an update earlier.''

Flynn nodded. "I'll bet he decided you weren't suitable, after all.''

She sucked in a long, irritable breath, but forced herself to smile. "That's right," she agreed sweetly. "Because I've been hanging around with you." A moment later she took her place beside her mother, as far from Flynn as it was possible to get in this intimate circle, and allowed herself a tiny sigh of relief.

The clergyman gathered the group closely together and began the traditional words of the wedding ceremony. Abbey took comfort in the familiar phrases. Old-fashioned they might be, but there was strength in the ritual.

She didn't intend to raise her eyes from the flowers she held, but she found herself studying Flynn as best she could from the corner of her eye. His hands were clasped together, his good hand unobtrusively giving support to the bandaged one. It worried her. Was the injury worse than he'd admitted?

"Frank's ring, Abbey," the clergyman said under his breath, and she fumbled to pull the gold band off her thumb, where it fitted so neatly, and handed it to him.

Janice's ring was in Flynn's coat pocket. He retrieved it on cue with no fuss at all. It was obvious to Abbey that he was having no trouble keeping his mind on the business at hand; he was practically a professional. Certainly his concentration hadn't been disturbed by what had happened between them earlier behind that row of boxwood.

What was she going to tell him?

The final blessing was given and the orderly, attentive group of friends collapsed into a laughing, hugging mob that made its way slowly back to the house and fell like a pack of locusts on the buffet tables.

Abbey put a sampling of hors d'oeuvres on her plate and took her seat next to Frank to listen to the toasts and the congratulations. Shrimp puffs, she thought, would never taste the same. There seemed to be something missing. . . .

But at least it was almost over; without a band or any other attraction to keep the guests entertained, they would start to drift away as soon as they had finished luncheon.

That wasn't a great deal of comfort, Abbey reminded herself. For then she'd have to face Flynn again.

She was still trying to figure out how long she could postpone that confrontation when the grand piano in the drawing room came softly to life with one of the most beautiful of the Strauss waltzes.

Janice's face lit with surprise and pleasure, and she turned to Frank. "Did you . . . ?"

"It was Flynn's idea," he said. "I thought you'd like it. Shall we dance?"

Of course, Abbey thought. It would be Flynn's idea.

She toyed with her coffee spoon and waited for the inevitable. The first waltz was always the bride and groom alone. The second would pair the family members, Janice with her new son and Abbey with Frank. Then as the bride and groom went on to dance with their friends, the best man and the maid of honor would take the floor together.

And there wasn't the smallest chance that Janice, for whom proper manners had always been as clear as Waterford crystal, would allow Abbey to forget it.

At the close of the second waltz, Wayne Marshall cut in to dance with Janice, and Flynn tapped his father on the shoulder. "Mine, I think," he said, and Abbey was left facing him.

"You're sure this won't hurt your hand?" she said feebly.

"Not unless you're planning to knock me down and step on it."

Abbey colored a little at the quizzical note in his voice. His bandaged hand came to rest lightly at her waist as the music started again. "What do you think of my brainstorm for a wedding gift? A pianist is much more original than a painting, don't you think?"

"I'm...surprised, that's all." What a mild way to put it, she thought. "You dance very well."

"My mother taught me."

The room was growing crowded with dancers, and Flynn drew her closer. His breath stirred the loose tendrils of hair at her temples.

Abbey closed her eyes tightly and let her head droop a little. If only she could be free to snuggle her face into his shoulder and really enjoy the warm strength of his arms around her....

The music shifted, and Abbey said huskily, "That's the end of the duty dance, you know."

"Oh, that's all right. I'm dancing with you because I don't want you to feel like a wallflower. A woman's extrasensitive right after she's been jilted, I know, and—"

"I was not—" Abbey stopped herself just in time. "I was not jilted exactly. It was more like a mutual agreement."

Wayne Marshall appeared beside him, and Flynn shook his head. "Not just now," he said, and before Abbey could debate the point, he had swept her off across the room.

"I'll just bet it was mutual," Flynn murmured. "Poor Boyd. It was only a summer romance, after all. Why did you tell him to take a hike, Abbey? Were you making room for me?"

Her gaze flashed up to meet his. "Why, you..."

The floor switched from smooth hardwood to paving brick as they glided through the French doors from drawing room to terrace. Abbey's high heel slipped in a low spot in the mortar, and Flynn drew her closer yet for support.

Her heart was pounding so hard she thought he must be able to feel its hammering against his chest.

"This was a hell of a bad idea," he murmured against her hair.

"You're absolutely right," Abbey said crisply. "Don't feel any obligation to—"

"The pianist, I mean. If it wasn't for my bright ideas, the party would be breaking up by now."

"It certainly wouldn't hurt my feelings any."

Flynn murmured, "And I could be off in a corner somewhere kissing you without an audience."

The idea was so inviting that for a moment Abbey could hardly breathe. She forced herself to be sensible. "I told you what happened this morning was a mistake, Flynn."

"In that case, perhaps we should try it again and see what you think this afternoon." His voice was no more than a rough whisper.

"This is indecent," she managed. "It's the middle of a wedding and you're trying to seduce me."

He smiled, and his arm tightened just a little, pulling her even closer. "Yes."

Abbey's breath caught. "We can't have an affair, Flynn."

"Really?"

He didn't sound very interested, and Abbey had to force herself to continue. She shook her head firmly. "It would hurt Mother and Frank, and—"

"No doubt about it. Still, you can't kiss a man like that and then tell him you goofed and expect him to forget it, Abbey. No, this time you've crossed the line."

Barely whispering, she said, "I'm sorry, Flynn, but—"

He smiled down at her and said calmly, "I'm not. Would you like to know what really happened to my hand?"

The abrupt shift almost stunned her. "I thought... You said you were pulling weeds."

He shook his head. "Merely a cover story. I forgot that back in the days when that blasted garage was built they still used real plaster, and the hard stuff at that. So when I slammed my hand into the wall..."

"On purpose?" Her voice was little more than a squeak. "Why?"

"Because for the last week I haven't painted a decent line. I can't even do grass anymore. Every damned thing I try to put on paper ends up looking like you."

Abbey's head was swimming, and she wasn't getting enough air. *This can't be real,* she told herself.

"But the final straw was that blasted shrimp puff." Their steps had grown steadily smaller and slower, and now they stopped dancing altogether. "When you started licking my fingers and didn't even notice that you were practically making love to me..."

I noticed, she thought. *I must have done too good a job of hiding it.*

"The longer I thought about it, the more frustrated I got. And ultimately I hit the wall." He shook his head ruefully.

"And what did that accomplish?"

"Not much. I stopped thinking about you, but only for a couple of minutes. I was afraid you were never going to stop flirting and let me get close enough again to convince you that we could have something special. Until this morning, when you finally stopped playing games and kissed me as if you honestly knew what you wanted." He cleared his throat and held her a little away from him. "All right," he said briskly. "We've agreed we can't have an affair because the parents would kill us. So what do you suggest we do, instead?"

Abbey tipped her head back and looked up at him. "Instead?" she said uncertainly.

His hands closed on her shoulders as if he were about to start shaking her. "You heard me, Abbey. What do you want?"

She picked out a stripe in his tie and stared at it. "I would like..." *To marry you. To be your love forever.*

But she couldn't say that. What if he didn't feel as strongly as she did? He had said they could have "something special." But he hadn't said he loved her, or that he wanted that special something to be permanent.

She swallowed hard and groped for words and finally remembered what he'd once said about the way he would approach someone he found very attractive. "I'd like for you to be a significant person in my life, Flynn."

He thought it over, and then he said almost gently, "No."

She looked up at him, eyes wide. "No?" Her throat was so dry she could hardly form the word.

"I won't settle for any less than being the *most* significant person in your life. For all your life, Abbey."

Relief surged through her, but she wasn't quite able to surrender just yet. "Don't get a big head," she recommended. "I still haven't really forgiven you for telling me that your greatest nightmare would be facing me across the dinner table every Christmas."

"Even though it was true?"

"Flynn!"

"Seeing each other on holidays, and no other time, and pretending it didn't matter..."

"It would have been unbearable," she admitted. "Did you know even then?"

"Not exactly. I just knew it didn't sound like a very good idea." He rubbed his cheek comfortably against her temple. "So what about it, Abbey? Shall we steal the parents' limelight and announce that we're getting married, too?"

Happiness flooded over her, and she flung herself against him with a glad little cry, arching her body against his and stretching to kiss him.

"Abbey, darling," he whispered against her lips.

"What?"

"People are watching. And you're not acting very suitably for a nice Armitage Road girl."

"Let them watch, dammit!"

Flynn smiled. "My point of view precisely," he murmured, and drew her even more tightly against him, so close that there wasn't room for Abbey to breathe. But that was all right, too, because the way he kissed her sent waves of pure oxygen racing through her body, enough

to make her light-headed and dizzy with relief and happiness.

There was a ripple of applause from the wedding
guests, but it didn't matter. Neither Flynn nor Abbey
heard it.

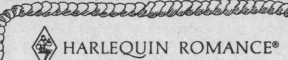 

Where do you find hot Texas nights, smooth Texas charm,
and dangerously sexy cowboys?

WHITE LIGHTNING

by Sharon Brondos

Back a winner—Texas style!

Lynn McKinney knows Lightning is a winner and she is
totally committed to his training, despite her feud with her
investors. All she needs is time to prove she's right. But
once business partner Dr. Sam Townsend arrives on the
scene, Lynn realizes time is about to run out!

CRYSTAL CREEK reverberates with the exciting rhythm of
Texas. Each story features the rugged individuals who live
and love in the Lone Star State. And each one ends with
the same invitation...

Y'ALL COME BACK...REAL SOON!

Don't miss WHITE LIGHTNING by Sharon Brondos.
Available in June wherever Harlequin books are sold.

Harlequin is proud to present our
best authors and their best books.
Always the best for your reading
pleasure!

Throughout 1993, Harlequin will bring you
exciting books by some of the top names in
contemporary romance!

In June,
look for
*Threats and
Promises* by

The plan was to make her nervous....

Lauren Stevens was so preoccupied with her new looks
and her new business that she really didn't notice a
pattern to the peculiar "little incidents"—incidents
that could eventually take her life. However, she did
notice the sudden appearance of the attractive and
interesting Matt Kruger who *claimed* to be a close
friend of her dead brother....

**Find out more in THREATS AND
PROMISES ... available wherever Harlequin
books are sold.**

BOB2

HARLEQUIN PRESENTS®

A Year DOWN UNDER

In 1993, Harlequin Presents celebrates the land down under. In June, let us take you to the Australian Outback, in OUTBACK MAN by Miranda Lee, Harlequin Presents #1562.

Surviving a plane crash in the Australian Outback is surely enough trauma to endure. So why does Adrianna have to be rescued by Bryce McLean, a man so gorgeous that he turns all her cherished beliefs upside-down? But the desert proves to be an intimate and seductive setting and suddenly Adrianna's only realities are the red-hot dust *and* Bryce....

Share the adventure—and the romance— of A Year Down Under!

Available this month in
A YEAR DOWN UNDER

SECRET ADMIRER
by Susan Napier
Harlequin Presents #1554
Wherever Harlequin books are sold.